Get first-hand r
updates about new relea.
and an exclusive **FREE eBook Box Set**
when you

JOIN MY VIP READER CLUB.

See back of book for details >>

ABOUT THE COLLECTION

Each book is a self-contained story and can be read as a standalone novel. However, they form part of a collection of stories that take place within the same time frame on the island of Lesvos.

Books in the Collection:

- Sealed with a Kiss
- A Change of Heart
- Eye of the Storm
- Sugar and Spice
- Amenah Awakens*

- The Sappho Romance (Alt. Hist. spinoff)

Free to VIP Reader Club.
See back of book for details >>

Sugar & Spice

Lesvos Island

SAM SKYBORNE

DUKEBOX.LIFE

Published by DukeBox.life.
http://DukeBox.life.

This is a work of fiction. Names, places and incidents are either products of the author's imagination or used fictitiously. Any resemblance to actual persons (living or dead), locales or events is purely coincidental.

Sam Skyborne asserts the moral right to be identified as the author of this work.

To all my fellow seekers who have found themselves in transition or on the brink of a new life in recent years.

1

*M*y bones felt like they were made of lead. I hadn't felt that tired since my late teens, when I had followed a girl up Snowdonia with no training in hiking. Nor girls, for that matter. It was truly amazing what one would do—correction, could do—in the name of love.

This time, however, love was not involved, not as much as spice, and not that kind of spice, either.

Although I was tired, and felt like I could sleep for a month, I felt good, proud, relieved and, ironically, light and free. I'd done well. It took me, if you count the rocky restarts, about six years to get there. The largest bone-crunching push had been in the last three months— the major drive to maximise the growth and sell the business for the most profit. It was touch and go, but that very day, I finally got a fat signature on a page, accompanied by an equally fat figure in my bank account.

Hence, I poured myself an enormous glass of the best red wine I had in my little cellar. I had been saving it specifically for that moment.

Most other people probably would have thrown a party or gone out on the razz. Under the circumstances, however, I was thrilled to have a relaxing evening in the company of my best friend. I could not want for anything more.

I realised I had poured a rather large glass. Jacko would most certainly have something to say about that. I smiled at the thought. I liked crystal, but the problem with this new crystal set was that each glass could probably hold an entire bottle, if one tried. Jacko already thought I was a glass snob. I probably was, and as I've told her before, there's no harm in that. I've never understood the appeal of thick-rimmed glasses—not on a face and not on the lips. Jacko often called me her "posh girl." I finally admitted she might be right about that, too.

I took my glass and my laptop over to the three-piece sofa in my living room.

My home was something I was quite proud of. It wasn't huge, since I didn't need very much, and one could say I favoured a very spartan decorating style. For me, the view spoke for itself and I didn't really need possessions to clutter the space. My apartment was on the top floor of a sky rise building in London on the north side, overlooking the Thames river. I had my own lift entrance on the ground floor, which prevented me from having to face the droves of people heading to the restaurant on one of the lower levels every time I came and went. The flat was a little on the pricey side, but it was worth it. Considering all the hours I spent elbow-high in spices, accounts, and business meetings, I needed something really worthy to show for it.

Now that I had sold the business, my life in all other ways felt even more empty than my living room and I couldn't really say why I had put in all those long hours, worked so hard, gave all my energy to a business, knowing that I would sell it one day. I was approaching forty. Some would say I gave the business the best years of my life and now, with the business gone, I had very little to show for it.

I didn't even have friends in the city I lived in. My best friend had settled on an island in Greece. There never seemed to be time or energy for developing luxuries like friendships. Occasionally, I would have a one-night stand if the opportunity arose, but even that was more to take the edge off than an attempt at anything more meaningful. I didn't even have a cat. Jacko asked me once how I could call myself a lesbian.

I sat down and tucked my legs underneath me, feeling the warm, soft suede of the couch envelop me. I rested the laptop on my leg and took a large sip of the velvety rich red wine before I hit the connect button.

The call connected and my computer screen lit up with the cute, slightly gruff, androgynous features of my best friend. I could see from Jacko's background that she was also settled on the couch in her living room in front of the open fire. Her house was in the village of Eressos on the western side of the island of Lesvos. I marvelled at the fact that no matter what time of year it was, she always looked like she had a golden-brown tan, even though she swore that for at least six months of the year, she never set foot on the beach.

"Hey, you," she said, the corner of her eyes wrinkling from her smile. She held a short tumbler of what I assumed, judging by the colour, was Metaxa.

"Here's to you, my friend. You have worked a long time for this. And now it's finally here. I am very, very proud of you." She raised her glass.

I matched her movements. It really was nice to celebrate like this with her. My only regret was that she wasn't with me in person.

"And here's to you, Jacko, for never losing faith in me and encouraging me every step of the way. If it wasn't for you, I certainly would never have got here."

Jacko smiled her sexy, skew smile. "Always." She raised her glass again before taking a large swig.

"So, what's next, my friend?"

"That's the big question. I now know what it feels like for a mother to have children move out of home for the first time. I feel like I've lost a limb."

"I guess it'll be hard for you to find a new balance after spending so much time in that business."

I had an idea. "I have a suggestion for you. Now that I have more time on my hands, why don't you come over and visit me for a while? I can show you London, well at least the bits of London I have come to know over the last few years."

Jacko guffawed in a hearty manner, as only she could. "In that case, I don't think we will leave the inside of your apartment."

I liked the direction the conversation was going in, even though I knew it was all meant innocently, but I would never admit that to Jacko. Not until I was absolutely sure that her intentions were as I understood them.

"You'd be surprised, my friend. I know a few other dives, too. Not all places you would necessarily want to go, mind, but at least it's more than my apartment." I took another sip of my wine, giving her time to consider my proposal.

Jacko took a large pull of her Metaxa.

I braced myself. I knew rejection was imminent. I still had to ask.

"Seriously, Jacko, how about coming to visit me? It would be a real boon to show you around London after all this time. I think we both deserve a break and a bit of balance."

"Shucks, Spice, man. That is such a fantastic invitation. Thank you. But you know me and the whole flying thing, man." She seemed genuinely regretful.

Yes, I did know how she was about flying. She was clinically phobic. I remembered suggesting a few years earlier that we go on a short break to the Galapagos. That definitely would have involved flying. She visibly blanched. She almost stopped breathing. The glass she had in her hand just about shattered in her grip. I realised then that it would take more than a miracle to get her onto a plane. Still, I thought it was worth trying on this occasion. Call me an incurable optimist.

The screen wobbled as Jacko leant forward. I could hear liquid being poured into a glass. I presumed she was topping her drink. She sat back and repositioned her laptop on her knee.

"I have a better idea," she said with an even bigger smile than before. "How about you come to me? Give yourself a break, a little reward. Come spend some time with me here, at my house. During the day, I will be out and about doing my chores and there are a few outdoor projects I have my eye on. That will keep me busy and give you enough time to unwind and relax, and then in the evenings, we can catch up."

Jacko had a very specialised and sought-after vocation, which allowed her to travel to all sorts of exotic places and gave her more than a very tidy income. We never talked about money but I gathered she could probably live on the proceeds from a single job for a couple of years, if she wanted. The rest of the time, she was an avid gardener and animal lover. She spent most of her free time growing greens and walking dogs and I loved her for that.

"Seriously, Spice, come visit me for a few days or weeks or months, however long you want. I think after all these years of putting all your energy into that business you, could do with the real, proper break with a good friend, warm sunshine, and vitamin D—the likes of which you haven't seen in a few years, judging by the veins visible through your skin."

I laughed, feeling my cheeks colour at the thought that Jacko might have looked at my body.

"The salty sea air and crisp, clear water would do you a lot of good," Jacko said. "It would give you some time to recuperate and decide what you would like to do with the rest of your life."

"Gosh, you make it sound like I'm about to be reborn."

"Well, are you not? Anyway, I know you better than to pressure you, so have a sleep on it tonight and then let me know. I'll make up the spare room, just in case."

I had to love Jacko. She did know me well enough to be presumptuous like that and get away with it.

"I will give it some thought." I felt a little discombobulated that she had turned the tables on me so easily, and I needed to change the topic. "So, tell me, where have you been this evening?"

I could always tell when Jacko was a little tiddled. Her evening had clearly started much earlier.

She smiled looking a little guilty. "We had our Greek evening."

I knew that Jacko regularly met with an expat group to practise their Greek speaking skills and learn about the Greek culture together.

"I was at Sophia and Giorgos' this evening with the girls. We watched the new *L Word* in Greek. That was quite an experience."

I laughed, wishing silently that I had a group of friends like that.

"Oh, yeah? You call that a Greek lesson? I can't imagine it. Though, that is one way to incentivise learning Greek."

"The sex scenes were about all I could understand," Jacko said, laughing.

I rolled my eyes. "Body language would be universal, I presume."

Jacko and I continued to chat for another hour, by which time, I could hardly keep my eyes open. I regretfully wished her a very good night and promised to give her suggestion some more thought the following day.

As soon as my head hit the pillow, I was out. The combination of extreme fatigue and the wine resulted in me sleeping for close to twelve hours solid. I woke up on Saturday morning slightly disorientated but feeling like a newborn with a new bounce to my step. On the way to getting coffee from the kitchen, I almost burst into a skip.

I sat on the balcony in the calm late morning sunshine sipping my coffee. The conversation with Jacko swirled in my head. Should I do it? Could I just up and go to Greece?

With the business wrapped up, I had no pressing reasons to stay in London. As a result of the money from the sale, I didn't even need to worry about renting out my apartment right away. I had been meaning to pay Jacko a proper, relaxed visit for a very long time. It would be nice to see her and really talk face to face for a change.

I drained my coffee.

Why the hell not?

ooking a plane ticket was actually quite a novel experience. Over the past few years, when my business was running at full throttle, I had a personal assistant, Gina, who did almost everything for me. I guess the clue is in the title. She would do everything from booking flights and accommodations, to making hair appointments, buying theatre tickets, making restaurant reservations, hiring cars, and organising a driver for me if I needed to have meetings en route. When I think about it, as I became more successful in business, I became almost incapable on so many other levels.

This time, I decided to do things differently. I took full responsibility for everything myself, and soon realised I actually enjoyed it and was not too bad at it. I even managed to find myself a direct flight to Mytilene.

On the evening of the flight, I caught the Stansted Express from Victoria. I thought I was clever to travel just after the rush hour to make sure I got a seat for what I expected to be a long journey. The joke was on me when we pulled into the airport station a mere half an hour later.

The train journey was long enough, though, for me to realise that I had grown so used to being pushed for time, rushed from pillar to proverbial post, that I had forgotten what it was like to sit on the train and observe the scenery passing me by. On this particular occasion, I was mesmerised by the late evening sunbeams being chopped up by the rapidly passing trees.

I usually travelled at the last minute, and Gina would hand me my boarding pass and instructions on how to bypass the queues at the security check just in time for take off. This time, I had reserved a hotel room for the night, but before I could relax, I needed to drop off my luggage at the check-in desk. There were no queues and the assistant behind the counter was very helpful—another delightful and unexpected experience for me.

The hotel reception area was a little busier and while I waited patiently for my turn to check in, I heard a high-pitched voice, tempered by a soft Scottish lilt, calling from the side of the reception area. "Ms Cox?"

I turned reluctantly.

"Ms Cox! It is you! I thought I recognised you." A worried looking blonde woman in a black-and-white hotel uniform rushed towards me. She came to an abrupt stop next to me and scanned her clipboard. "I'm so sorry, Ms Cox, you are not on my list. I don't know what happened..."

I smiled my most disarming smile and checked her name tag.

"Roselind," I said, saying the name clearly with enough inflection to encourage correction in case I got the pronunciation wrong.

The younger woman nodded.

"It's okay, Roselind. I won't be on there. I'm not travelling for business this time. However, you might have a Terry Spice on your list."

Roselind frowned again. Then she seemed to pick up on my meaning. She glanced around the hotel's lobby to check that nobody was listening. I was sure, especially after her calling to me across the reception, that all eyes were now on us, but I smiled again.

Despite insisting that I didn't want a fuss, Roselind took me aside and checked me in as a VIP guest. I figured that since my anonymity had already been blown, I had might as well relent and let her help and get this part over with as quickly as possible. I hoped to blend in later. However, I noticed Roselind checking conspicuously on me for the duration of the evening.

It was not as if I were a celebrity. The problem was not that anyone would particularly recognise me. The unwanted attention was from having a certain busy business focussed lifestyle. This time, I just wanted to do what everyone else does.

Even though I had access to a double en suite for the nine-hour sojourn before my flight, I decided to spend the evening in the lounge, where I could soak up the atmosphere and people watch in the Tower Bar—so named on account of the very large blue honeycomb-esque tower of wine bottles that extended from the ground floor up towards the third-floor ceiling. A young, very fit looking girl in a black leotard and tights sailed up and down on trapeze wires, collecting and returning wine bottles as orders were placed at the bar. This not only provided a very pleasant, mesmerising focal point, it also provided an ample incentive for expensive wine orders. More so, it provided an easy conversation starter with fellow travellers with a few idle hours to kill.

It was exactly that which brought a young Australian poet named Erica to my attention. She was a very beautiful, quirky young woman with deep chocolate brown eyes and a warm, sunny smile like her home country. A glass and a half of overly expensive wine later, I realised I had been completely reeled in by her vibrant, youthful, and quite refreshing take on the world, politics, and art. It had been a long while since I had mixed with younger adults like Erica. I had spent most of my recent years in pretentious boardrooms or sick high-rise offices, with corporate execs and stuffy has-been entrepreneurs. At about 10:45 p.m., Erica packed up her things. It turned out she sadly was not spending the night with me or even in the hotel. Instead, she was heading out on the last flight to Munich, where she was meeting a group of her friends from her university days for Oktoberfest.

How marvellous it must be to have a group of friends you had made at the beginning of life's journey, before things got complicated and political and you grew old and cynical. The only friend I had kept from my younger years was Jacko.

Jacko and I met one drunken weekend in Ibiza, where we were the only girls on the island not overtly looking for their Adonis. Rather, she was an out butch baby dyke at that stage and I was 'confused'. I had always felt more comfortable in a frock than DMs, perhaps because I was more susceptible to the pressure to conform, unlike Jacko. But my sexuality was always clear to me, anyway.

I ordered another glass of wine and sat back, wallowing in the nostalgia of that first night with Jacko. There was nothing sexual about that night, or any other night, with her. To be honest, I had never really allowed myself to entertain the thought of anything other than Jacko being my best friend.

It had been my first night on the island. After a day in the hot basking sun, wearing little in the way of protection beyond a flimsy sundress and dark glasses, I had been strong-armed to join in by a crowd of fellow students who were heading to a local nightclub. Three strong Porn Star cocktails in, I had wobbled my way to the toilets, reaching the cubicle just in time to not embarrass myself. I projectile vomited the said three cocktails into the toilet bowl. However, in my haste, I had forgotten to close the cubicle door behind me. So, after what seemed like an age of unpleasant retching, I was startled by the deep tones of a Greek accent from close behind me. I spun round so quickly that I lost my footing and slipped. If Jacko had not caught me, I could have probably broken my skull on the porcelain bowl of the toilet, a fact I only realised much later. I was instantly taken by her deep brown eyes and firm hands as she lowered me gently to the floor. I remembered thinking, *if only I was not sitting on the floor with my head resting on the side of a toilet bowl, I could ask her name and telephone number.* Before I could act on that, I was overcome by another wave of alcohol pushing at my diaphragm.

Luckily for me, Jacko took her chivalry very seriously. Once I was sure there was nothing left in my stomach, she helped me up and guided me to the basin to wash up.

"Some fresh night air and a little exercise always helps me feel better when my poison bites back," she'd said and lead me outside for a walk.

I have no idea what we talked about for the two hours we wandered around along the coast of San Antonio. Whatever it was, it was the beginning of a beautiful, decade-long friendship that had seen me through thick and thin—from being the retching fish out of water in a nightclub, to pursuing my dream of running a successful international business, to now—the end of an era and hopefully the start to a new phase in my life.

I raised my glass to myself. "To whatever comes next," I said.

The flight to Mytilene took just under four hours and passed without incident. As the plane descended towards the dusty cement runway of Mytilene Airport, I was struck by the saturated quality of light this late in the season, and even though I knew to expect it, the hot, humid midday heat hit my lungs hard.

I stepped out of the plane and, along with the handful of other travellers, made my way to the bus that ferried us the short distance to the Arrivals terminal.

The new border passport control ran slowly but smoothly and I didn't have to wait long before my suitcase appeared through the rubber curtain on the conveyor belt.

As soon as I exited the airport, a swarm of sweaty, bearded taxi drivers descended on me, demanding exorbitant fares to take me to my destination. However, one quick sweep of my surroundings and my eyes landed on Jacko, leaning casually against the dusty bonnet of her small white Fiat. Dressed in jeans and a tight white T-shirt that showed off her defined deltoids, she looked fresh, cool and collected. Unlike the rest of the impatient crowd, in true Jacko style, she stood waiting for life—and me—to come to her. That set off a slight flutter in my stomach.

When she spotted me, her face lit up, accentuating the laughter lines around her eyes. She flicked her cigarette butt to the floor and in a slow, deliberate movement, stubbed it out with her cowboy boot. She reminded me of a Greek, female John Wayne, but rather than being comical, it suited her. In three large steps, we collided in the warmest, biggest, most engulfing hug I'd had had in years. It felt like our souls connected. I had heard of people talking about a feeling of coming home in a spiritual or emotional way when they reconnected with their loved ones. That moment was the closest I had ever come to such a feeling.

"You look awesome, as always." Her deep voice stroked my soul.

Jacko took my suitcase and hoisted it into the boot of her car. It looked huge in the small vehicle and it made me feel awkward, like I had overpacked despite it only being a cabin-size case. It reminded me that Greek island living demanded little as a holiday destination. You needed little more than a toothbrush, bikini, and a clean pair of underwear. More important was to bring a broad smile and a healthy sense of adventure.

"So, I was wondering, unless you're too tired and would rather go straight home, whether you'd like to have lunch somewhere on the way?" Jacko asked, as she started the engine.

There was no way I was ready to go home. I was wired. What was it with all these girlish jitters, I wondered. Perhaps I was finally beginning to realise the enormity of this new stage in my life.

Jacko drove us to a lovely little village on the south coast of the island, just beyond Kalloni, called Apothikes. Here, there was only one tavern at the head of a small jetty in the bay, where several tiny fishing boats lay moored, gently bobbing in the calm water. One of the boats Jacko pointed out was barely bigger than a bathtub. It was tiny and she told me that its Greek name on the side of the hull meant 'giant'. This caused us more happy giggles.

The restaurateur, an older woman with a kind face, came out to greet us. Since she only spoke Greek, Jacko took charge and ordered us a spread of small Greek dishes to sample and a couple of cold beers.

Even though we video-called at least once a week, we still had so much to chat about. It was nice to communicate in full 3D face-to-face reality and not to be hampered by the electronic, two-dimensional restrictions of a computer screen and dodgy data rates.

"So, how is Jacko world?" I asked after we'd ordered a second beer.

I watched as Jacko took a long pull from her cigarette. "Ah, you know. Life is life." She shrugged her shoulders and flicked the ash off the tip of the cigarette before taking another long pull.

"Come on, Jacko, give a little. It's been such a long time since I saw you and I didn't come all this way for 'life is life' platitudes. Tell me, how are you really? You're talking to me, Spice. Is there someone?" The moment the words left my mouth, I regretted them. I had not realised that this was the burning question on my mind, and now, finally having asked it, I dreaded to hear the answer.

"Ah, Spice, man, you know me," she shrugged again.

"I do know you."

We both laughed.

"So, tell me."

Jacko grew serious, and my chest tightened.

"There is someone?" My voice hitched, and I hoped to God she had not noticed.

Her brown eyes met mine, and a slight flush crept over her suntanned skin. For a moment, the way she held my gaze allowed me to hope. It was only a moment, but it was enough to make her next words feel like a rusty, blunt dagger that ripped through my heart.

"Her name is Beers."

Jacko proceeded to tell me about her. She was a young English girl, who had come to Skala hoping to get away from an old life.

Don't we all.

For the next twenty minutes, Jacko talked about this girl, most of

15

which drifted over me like a cool mist, nebulous and intangible. All I could think, like a stuck record, was, *What kind of name is Beers?*

Some time later, the restaurateur came to check if we wanted a last drink. They were getting ready to close. We had spent the better part of six hours there. I paid our bill, and we left for Jacko's home in the Kampos, just outside Skala Eressos.

Being one of the first lesbians to make their permanent home in Skala Eressos, Jacko was lucky enough to get her hands on one of the solid stone-built houses in the Kampos. It was a beautiful, double-story house with two large double rooms upstairs. Downstairs had an open-plan kitchen and living room complete with hearth and adjacent bathroom. The house benefited from 360-degree windows, which meant it could catch the sun and the shade all year round. A friend of hers, who was a horticulturalist, had designed her a secluded courtyard with deciduous foliage that would bloom in summer, providing cool thick shade in the harsh hot Greek summer sunshine. In winter, the foliage died away and let in the welcome winter warmth.

3

*J*acko had thoughtfully anticipated that I'd be tired after my travels, so rather than dragging us out for dinner, she had prepared a lovely meal of lamb, tzatziki, and my favourite Greek baked aubergine, *imam*. We had a quiet dinner together. By then, my initial excitement and giddiness had subsided and given way to a more low-key, somewhat subdued mood. If Jacko had noticed, she didn't ask about it. She probably assumed that I was merely fatigued. I didn't disabuse her.

At about 10:30 p.m., I excused myself as graciously as I could. I was very careful not to let on that there was anything wrong. My emotional reaction to Jacko's news surprised even me. It all felt very raw. I needed time to think, and I wasn't ready to answer questions I didn't even know the answers to. I also didn't want her to doubt whether I wanted to be there.

When I got to my bedroom, I didn't have the energy to unpack. I took out my toiletries and my pyjamas and a few of the bare essentials, more to give the impression that I was trying to sort myself out than to actually do anything functional. I had a quick shower to wash away the day's travel dirt, and brushed my teeth before I crawled into bed. My brain was not big enough to cope with any more input, so I promptly turned off the light.

Lying in the cool, almost cold, early October darkness of Jacko's spare bedroom, I listened to the sounds of her moving around the house, clearing up the kitchen, banking the fire.

I finally allowed myself a moment of honest reflection. Instantly, my eyes grew moist, and I could feel the emotions swirl and gather like a rising flood. Until that moment, I had not acknowledged exactly how devastated I was about the news that Jacko had someone. Why would it bother me so much?

I tried to remember Jacko's description of Beers, of this person who had captured her heart. If I remembered correctly, she sounded so familiar, so much like me. Or was that just my own wishful thinking? I recollected sitting in the tavern opposite Jacko, unconsciously holding my breath, waiting as she described this person. and I found myself wishing that she would end her description with 'and this person is you.' Of course, those words never came.

Now, there I was, lying in the dark, on my own. I knew it wasn't rational, but I felt like I'd lost, not only an opportunity for happiness, but I felt petrified that I was also about to lose my friend.

Finally, the house went quiet. I was acutely aware of Jacko in the room next to me and the thought occurred to me: What if I just got up and went to her room right now and told her how I felt? Would she welcome me into her bed with open arms? I tried to imagine it.

For the first time in my life, I allow myself to imagine what it would be like to be with Jacko. Given that most of my time had been taken up by boardrooms, meetings, PowerPoint presentations, and wheeling and dealing in the spice trade, I'd had little experience with women, outside of the occasional one-night stand. The spice trade left little time for any other spice in my life.

I tried to imagine what it would be like to hold Jacko's hand like a girlfriend would, to feel the warmth of her artisan hands on my smooth pale skin. Despite my lack of experience, my imagination soon filled in the blanks and embellished the story until, without deciding to do so, I started to touch myself. I imagined the warmth of her breath on my cheek. The faint aroma of the Metaxa on her breath as she leant in close to me. The soft, warm feeling of her lips on mine. Her reassuring, strong arms enveloping me, but above all, the look in her eyes—a look that had no words, yet conveyed everything with such intensity that it burned into my soul, igniting a deep desire and passion I had repressed so effectively for too long.

My fingers slipped between my folds, wet, drenched with desire. I pulled the pillow over my head, knowing I would be incapable of suppressing my cries. It only took a few swift strokes of my fingers against my sensitive flesh for me to come. Spasms racked through my body as pleasure rolled over me like crashing waves.

I allowed myself to drift in that sweet oblivion for as long as I could and hold back all rational thought.

All too soon, the thought of going to Jacko's room drifted back. I imagined finding the room dark and unfamiliar, and tripping over items on the floor. Then Jacko waking up and mistaking me for an intruder, whacking me over the head with the large golden ornamental dildo on her nightstand—the very same one I had brought back for her as a joke from the Penis God Temple in Taiwan a few years previously.

I suppressed a scoff and wiped my tear-drenched cheeks.

I lay there in a pool of my sweat—damp, cooling, chilling. My comic musings soon descended into a depression as I admitted to myself that Jacko and I will never be anything more than what we were.

I had known Jacko for over a decade now and never once had she showed an interest in me, not even during drunken, intimate evenings when our conversations lent themselves to the most raw and revealing confessions. Even if—and it was a most improbable if—she felt something for me, the practical part of me had to admit that a relationship between us would never work. My life was in England. Her life was in Greece. Even though I was now technically a free agent, I was only free from my business. My world, my identity, my connections, and what was left of my family were all in England.

I scoffed again. Jacko wouldn't even fly…

We would end up the pen-pal or zoom-buddy versions of Vita Sackville West and Violet Trefusis. I tried to imagine Jacko and I engaging in zoom sex. I was relieved to find that my macabre sense of humour had not yet deserted me.

I took a deep breath and dried my tears on my sheet. I was never one to entertain a lengthy wallow. My grandmother used to say, "Nothing good came from a pity party. It is what you do because of the pain that counts."

She was right. But here there was nothing to be done. It was what it was. Jacko was my best friend and for as long as I had anything to do with it, or any say in the matter, I would hang on to that for dear life.

The fact was, I was there. I had come to Greece to see Jacko as a way to transition to a new life, into a new phase. God only knew what that would entail. But I was certain it would never include a relationship between Jacko and me, so I resolved to make the most of this time with my mate. Who knew? I might even find somebody else I vaguely liked on the island.

The following day, Jacko and I spent most of the time relaxing at her home. While she tended the garden, I sat on the veranda, wrapped up in my winter woollies and a windproof anorak that I had borrowed from her. I had found a sheltered sunny corner where I could soak up the weak but bright autumn sunshine. She had made a warm Winter Pimm's punch—a special treat since I liked Pimm's in the UK. I tried to explain that, although I was grateful, I was in Greece and hoped to make a point of experiencing all things Greek. She agreed to make some Rakomelo next time.

The following evening was Greek night. It was the regular 'learn the Greek language and culture in a fun way' night, hosted by Jacko's friends, Sophia and Giorgos. Sophia and Giorgos were both Greek and very proud of their culture and language. When they started making friends with several expats who had moved to Eressos, they took it upon themselves to host these evenings to help their friends learn Greek and find out about the rich Greek culture. It also probably helped that Sophia had lived in London for a few years and knew from personal experience how hard it was to get to grips with a new language and new culture adequately in order to make a life in a foreign country.

As soon as we arrived at the party, it became clear very quickly that Sophia and Giorgos were also the only straight people there. The rest of the thirty-something attendees seemed to be all lesbian expats from the British Isles, Germany, and The Netherlands.

Sophia and Giorgos had prepared a wonderful spread of Greek canapés and drinks to lubricate the event.

"Welcome," Sophia said. "Here, have an ouzo."

I was not sure whether to have one, not being a great fan of aniseed.

"Really, I recommend it. Especially if you're going to try out your Greek. Ouzo loosens the tongue," Sophia said.

"And the inhibitions," Giorgos added, kissing Sophia on the cheek and slapping her playfully on the bottom.

I was introduced and shown about a bit like a suitcase on a conveyor belt—far too fast to actually remember more than a handful of names—but the sentiment meant a lot. I hoped to at least recognise some faces when I saw them again.

Everyone seemed friendly and welcoming. Rather than a social gathering of acquaintances, it felt more like a large family occasion. The air seemed to crackle with excitement and friendship as people caught up with their week's activities and news. Some even tried to do it in Greek.

"It's lovely that everyone is so friendly and all seem to get on so well," I whispered to Jacko when we finally had a few minutes to ourselves.

"Don't be fooled," Jacko said. "There are a lot of undercurrents." She chuckled. "You'll no doubt find that out for yourself as you spend more time here."

"Greek small talk over canapés" was followed by contemporary disco. In that part of Greece, 'contemporary' included mostly eighties and nineties music. At one point, Jacko grabbed my arm and dragged me into the area of the courtyard that was the designated dance floor. Luckily, by then, the three glasses of wine I had consumed had loosened my limbs and my inhibitions sufficiently for me to not look like Pinocchio trying to break-dance to "The Dancing Queen."

In the middle of that dance, I suddenly realised that I was actually having fun—for the first time in a very, very long while.

Almost as abruptly, the music changed from bouncing pop to the slow pulsing rhythms of Macy Gray's "I Try". Before I could retreat, Jacko took my hand and pulled me into her, and we started slow dancing together, our bodies inches apart and our pelvises swaying in unison to the chorus, "I play it off but I am dreaming of you."

I became aware of how close we were. I felt a sudden urge to lean forward and kiss her. Everything felt so comfortable, so close that a kiss felt like the natural, inevitable next step. Thankfully, just before I did, a loud crash stopped us in mid-motion.

I turned to see what had happened. A woman whom I did not know had stumbled into a cluster of bottles on a side table, sending a tray of eats and the bottles crashing to the floor.

Saved by the bell, I bolted and stumbled back to where we had been standing near the main eats table.

As I pushed my way from the dance-floor, the spectators began to applaud. Our dance moves had apparently caught the attention of the crowd and the moment I stepped away they started lobbying for more.

When Jacko had finally finished taking her bows, lapping up the attention, showman that she was, she came to find me at the drinks table, where I was pouring myself another glass of retsina with shaky hands.

"Are you okay?" Jacko asked.

I took a large sip of my drink and nodded, the sharp taste of the liquid catching me in the back of the throat.

"Yes," I choked. "I just needed a drink. I'm not as fit as I thought." I tried to sound light-hearted.

"Retsina is perhaps not the best way to quench your thirst," Jacko said, gently slapping me on my back as I continued to cough.

Just then, a tall redheaded woman came over and grabbed Jacko by the arm. "Jacko, come. Show me some of those moves," she said in a thick Polish accent.

Jacko mouthed "excuse me," looking apologetic as she allowed herself to be dragged to the dance-floor.

I didn't mind. I was relieved to have a few minutes to myself to recover, and was quite content standing there minding my own business.

"So, are you Jacko's new girl?"

The question came out of nowhere and I almost choked on my drink again. I turned to find that a short peroxide-blonde woman with aqua blue eyes and a compact athletic build had sidled up next to me. I could not help frowning at the rather abrasive question.

"Oh, I'm sorry. That must seem like a very direct and personal question from somebody whose name you don't even know."

"I'd say."

The young woman jabbed her hand towards me. "The name is Rebecca. Most people call me Becks."

Considering her rather forward manner, I wasn't sure whether to respond, but in the friendly spirit of the evening I took her hand, making sure not to give her a knuckle cruncher, nor present a wet fish.

"Terry. My friends call me Spice." I couldn't help the slightly ambivalent tone that crept into my voice.

"Well, Spice," she said deliberately, "nice to meet you."

I took another sip of my drink.

"I apologise for my directness. I'm from Australia originally. Way, way back. I guess it comes with the territory." She allowed a slight Ozzy twang to slip into her accent. "I meant nothing disrespectful." She held up her hands. "So, are you? I mean, it's not a judgement. Or, wait let me guess. You two are longtime exes. Either way, it's cool. I just don't want to step on any toes. I'm not really keen on dirty laundry or on recycling, if you get my drift."

I really had no idea what she was on about, and for a moment, I wasn't quite sure whether we were actually having the same conversation.

"Well, you clearly know each other very well, judging from that." She nodded in the direction of the dance-floor.

I shook my head. "No, we are not exes, nor currently involved." I was suddenly aware of the lump forming in my throat.

"Honest mistake." She held up her hands again. "If you know Jacko, then you must know that she hardly leaves any stone unturned and from past experience, it's best to ask straight up."

At this point, I was starting to wonder if somebody had spiked my drink.

However, my answers seemed to please Becks, as her face had lit up, revealing an unexpectedly cute dimple in each cheek. It occurred to me she probably had practiced that smile and kept it in a finely tuned arsenal of moves and gestures designed to turn her prey.

"I can ask you the same question," I heard myself say.

Becks frowned and shook her head. "Jacko is not my 'cup of tea', as you English say."

Both the distinction that she did not identify as English, despite the slight Yorkshire twang interlaced with a fluent Australian accent, and the matter-of-fact rejection of Jacko made me wonder even more about her.

She was a short, sporty looking woman. Her shoulder-length blonde hair was styled into an androgynous undercut and she clearly could handle herself comfortably in queer circles. However, she also struck me as a person who could be equally at ease on the arm of a rich toy boy.

She caught me studying her, but rather than display signs of embarrassment, she smiled wickedly and winked at me. I could feel myself blush and tried to look casual while frantically trying to think of a way to change the topic.

"In that case, how long are you here for?" she asked, ignoring my obvious discomfort. "Maybe, when Jacko is busy, I can show you around. Would be good to get a different perspective on island life." She gave me another one of her dimpled smiles, and it occurred to me that for the first time in a very long time, I was actually being flirted with. The thought felt strange, like a marshmallow with a pebble inside it—both sweet and salty, weird but not entirely unpalatable.

I nodded, without giving it much thought.

I noticed the music had changed, and I saw Jacko bow theatrically at her dance partner.

"Right, that's my cue," Becks said. "I'll leave you two to catch up. It's time for a refill." She ducked away before I could answer.

4

_____

*D*espite the party ending late, and me still not having fully recovered from the flight, I woke up before dawn and rather than fighting the daylight, I got up and slipped out for a walk.

My meandering carried me down the hill, towards Skala Eressos. The beach was beautiful. The sea was a pure reflection of the sky, a calm, silky silver blue.

There were people out enjoying the early morning already. One gentleman was practicing the sun salutation in nothing more than his beard. A woman was trawling the shallows for knickknacks and pebbles. Neither seemed to notice me. They reminded me a little of my recent self—single-minded in their pursuits. How many years had I had laser focus on a single endeavour, to the exclusion of all else, missing out on so many other valuable experiences?

Numerous dog walkers were out, making use of the quiet time in the early part of the day to let their dogs off-lead.

About halfway down the beach, near an abandoned volleyball court, I came to a stop. The air was not warm, but I felt an overwhelming urge to strip off and immerse myself in the mercurial sea. It was truly breath taking.

By the time I got back to the house, Jacko was up and had gone to the local baker to buy the most delicious freshly baked German bread. Again, it struck me as odd to have German bread on a Greek island. However, despite how delicious and healthy Greek food was, as a permanent resident on the island, perhaps one occasionally fancied something different.

Over a cup of strong coffee and a piece of the bread, Jacko informed me of the few errands she had to run during the early part of the day, but promised to take me to lunch at Liotta. She offered to invite a few of her friends to join us. She wanted to introduce me to her social circle as part of showing me her life. In truth, all I really wanted to do was spend time with Jacko on her own, to catch up with my friend. Even though we had been having video calls on a regular basis, I didn't feel we were as close as we could be. Although I did not voice that, I think she seemed pleased that I had opted to have lunch with just her.

After lunch, we returned to Jacko's terrace.

"It seems like life here consists of pastry-breakfast, too-strong coffee, a dip in the sea, followed by a lunch banquet accompanied by the free flow of wines and ouzo at one or other of the spectacular Greek Tavernas. To be followed by a much-needed recovery nap to regain the energy to start again with a feast from mid-evening, followed by partying till the small hours."

I picked up my glass of Prosecco and sipped it, turning my head to face the late afternoon sunshine. I realised that what I had said could unintentionally present as criticism.

"Don't get me wrong, it's truly wonderful," I patted my bulging tummy, "but if I keep going like this, I will be the size of a house."

I always liked hearing Jacko's sexy, deep chuckle. It reminded me of hot chocolate on a winter's afternoon, soothing and nourishing to the soul.

"I guess unless you have a job or a calling, life here can be pretty simple," she nodded, "and that is why I like it."

Just then, Jacko's phone vibrated on the table between us. She glanced at the incoming number. I saw her expression change from lazy and sun soaked to attentive and focussed.

"Sorry, I've got to take this," she said and got up, stepping away to the edge of the terrace.

For the next ten minutes, I observed Jacko pacing back and forth along the terrace, talking into the phone excitedly in Greek.

"Μπορώ να επισκευάσω το Stradivarius, αλλά δεν πετάω για Μόσχα!" Jacko said, in a very emphatic tone.

Of course, I couldn't understand what she was saying, other than the odd recognisable English words like, "Stradivarius" and "Moscow". When the call ended, Jacko turned to me with a serious look on her face. She ran her hand through her curly dark hair, a gesture I was quite familiar with. It normally meant some discomfort.

"Unfortunately, I have to go to work tomorrow," she said.

That caught me off guard. "Work?"

Jacko was a musical instrument specialist. Specifically, a stringed instrument engineer. She was brilliant at what she did—one of the two best in the world. Because of the specialised and highly lucrative nature of her occupation, actual jobs were few and far between, allowing her to live the lazy life she desired in relative luxury on a Greek island the rest of the time.

On this occasion, the client was an obscenely wealthy Russian oligarch, a Count, for whom she regularly serviced his private collection of stringed instruments, including five out of the 650 surviving original Stradivari instruments.

Jacko needed to go to Moscow as soon as possible. The problem, and the reason for her emphatic tone earlier, was that Jacko did not fly.

This made travelling for her quite a complicated and lengthy prospect. Even the offer by the oligarch's personal assistant to send His Illustrious Highness's private jet to pick her up in Mytilene, or even his helicopter, which would pick her up from the beach in Skala Eressos, fell on deaf ears.

"If he wants me, he'll have me when I get there," Jacko simply concluded, without an ounce of hubris.

"When will you go?" I asked, trying to absorb this sudden news.

"I leave on the ferry tomorrow morning."

"Wow, so soon?"

Jacko shrugged and gave me her "it cannot be helped" shrug.

Of course I knew she had to go. However, I couldn't help feeling a little disappointed. Now, when I finally had time to see Jacko, her work, of all things, was taking her away.

We had a very lovely evening together, despite Jacko needing to pack and prepare for her trip. Unlike me, who would fret for hours about my wardrobe, which toiletries to include, and whether I had digital and paper copies of all my documents, Jacko seemed to take packing for the trip to the Count's visit like she was going to overnight in the next-door village. She even had time to cook us the most exquisite stew for dinner.

I had offered to take her to the ferry terminal in the morning. That meant a very early rise. Typically, she insisted on driving us there. That meant that after waving her off, I only had to navigate myself back to Skala Eressos. On the way there, Jacko had explained that she had told Sophia and Giorgos that I would attend the next Greek evening on my own and that they should look out for me.

"I can look after myself, Jacko." I tried to reassure her. However, I realised it was her need, or her guilt at leaving right now, that was at play. There was no point in arguing. Although Jacko was a force to be reckoned with, I had learnt a long time ago that one doesn't always have to put up a fight to have control of your own destiny.

5

*A*t 7:00 p.m. on the evening of the Greek event, Sophia herself arrived at Jacko's door. I was about to protest that I preferred a quiet night in, but Sophia would have none of it. Instead, she waited for me to get ready and then walked me all the way to their house, where she handed me an enormous glass of wine and reintroduced me to the people who were already milling about, poring over the delicacies she and Giorgos had prepared.

Everybody greeted me with broad smiles and eager nods, but after initial pleasantries, the conversation ran dry and I reverted to the well-practiced mode of looking busy doing nothing. A younger person would probably have resorted to scrolling through mundane social media posts on their phones. Not being a social media fan, I considered feigning an urgent call. However, I could not think of any appropriate pressing reason that could call me away right then. Besides, a rapid departure would certainly get back to Jacko and elicit a telling off. All I could do was endure a little longer until it was a socially acceptable time to leave.

"Hello again."

The sudden voice so close next to me startled me. I turned and saw the familiar dimples.

"You know, you really should not creep up on people like that. You could risk having a white wine shower." I indicated the almost empty glass I was holding.

"I was just wondering if you could do with a refill," Becks said.

I nodded.

She turned to the drinks table against which I had been leaning. It looked rather bare with only two bottles of white wine and what Sophia had told me was a home-brewed cider in a ceramic jug.

I drained my glass of wine and then reached for the cider to try it.

"Ooh, I would not do that if I were you."

I paused.

"Unless, of course, you want a mouth that feels like dried apples and a head that feels like it has been through the apple press in the morning."

I put the jug down. We studied the two bottles of wine. Neither looked impressive, but, then, I was not really familiar with Greek wines. I knew two names of reasonably good inexpensive wines that Jacko had introduced me to and I tended to stick with them.

"What do you say we nip out and get a bit of fresh air and something decent to drink?"

For a moment, I didn't respond, mostly trying to figure out what a "bit of fresh air" could mean, since we were already standing outside.

She laughed—a bubbly chuckle. "I don't bite…much."

That made me laugh, too. *What the hell, why not.* I put my glass down and followed her.

We slipped out the side entrance of the courtyard. Neither of us said goodbye to anyone. For a moment, I worried it might seem rude, but then I reassured myself that everyone looked busy and no one would miss me. After all, we probably wouldn't be long. A quick drink with

Becks had to beat standing around pretending not to be a wallflower.

I followed Becks quite a way down the road and then around the corner into a darker alley. I was beginning to wonder what type of bar could possibly be down such a narrow alley when we came to a stop next to a red and blue scooter. Becks took out a key from her rucksack and got onto the bike. She shoved the bike forward to take it off its stand, and started it up. The noise of the engine in the narrow alley was louder than I'd expected.

"Come on, then," she shouted over the rumble, "hop on!"

I was about to protest. First, I don't make a habit of getting on a bike, let alone without the correct protective gear. Secondly, she didn't mention taking me off somewhere farther than we could walk.

"Isn't there a taverna in the village we could go to?"

"Not unless you fancy more vinegar to drink."

I was about to object that surely not all Greek tavernas served acidic wine.

"Come on. Where's your sense of adventure?"

I frowned. "Can't we walk? I am not great on two wheels."

She turned off the bike engine, clearly tired of shouting. "We can. However, it's about a thirty-minute walk from here." She paused. "On the bike it takes a little over five, maybe ten minutes, if I take it real slow."

I hesitated.

"Come on, live a little. I promise I'll make it worth it." In the dim streetlight, I could see she was flashing me her dimples again and my mind went into a complete stall.

Despite my better judgement, I stepped forward and grabbed hold of her shoulder. She braced the bike, holding it steady as I swung my leg over the back and got on behind her.

"Ready?"

Not at all, I thought, but nodded.

She started the engine and pulled off with a slight jerk, causing me to grab on tight around her waist.

We headed down the road towards the sea and I presumed she was heading to Skala Eressos. At the large tree, the site of the turnoff to Mytilene, she took a left turn and headed up the incline, taking us farther out of town. I tried not to worry or second-guess our destination, but just focus on not bouncing off the back of the scooter as we bumped along the rough, potholed road. The scooter, clearly not designed for a heavier load, sounded like a bee in a biscuit tin, straining to drag us up the incline.

Becks slowed the scooter and took another sharp left turn onto a gravel road, leaving even the sparse streetlights behind, and soon we had only the stars and what seemed like a somewhat insipid, loose, bobbing scooter headlamp lighting our way.

Eventually, we crossed what I could only guess was a bridge over something and then, to my alarm, Becks slowed down and manoeuvred the scooter over to the side of the road, where she cut the engine.

"See, not far," she said. I realised she was waiting for me to get off.

I tried to dampen down my now-rampaging sense of panic. Which bar could possibly be out here?

Once I was clear of the motorbike, she heaved the machine onto its stand.

I tried to see into the dark and get some bearing of where I was.

"Come on, then," she said cheerfully as she stepped off the road and seemingly into a bush.

"Where are we?" I ventured forward, trotting to catch up with her. The last thing I wanted was to be stranded alone, God and Becks only knew where.

"You'll see," she called back.

It was only once I had lost complete sight of the road and the bike that I realised she was following some sort of narrow track.

This far away from any light pollution, the moon looked dazzling. It illuminated the surrounding hills, but I still did not know where we could possibly be headed. There did not seem to be any sign of civilisation anywhere nearby.

I was now seriously starting to wonder if I had done the right thing to come away with this woman. What if she was a serial killer with a history of luring other women away and then murdering them in a dark, remote hideout in the country? Her backpack, which I had squeezed to my chest between us for most of the journey, was not enormous. I tried to remember if I had felt the hard edges of a weapon or firearm. She certainly was not wearing bulky enough clothes under which to conceal one on her person.

Maybe she was a black belt or something and able to kill people with her bare hands. Or an assassin? Who would want me dead? My mind was running riot.

I remembered us standing at the drinks table in Sophia and Giorgos' courtyard and recollected that she was quite short, at least an inch shorter than me. That must be an advantage I could use, certainly if I keep to the high ground above her.

Surely it was very rare that a woman turned out to be a rapist or a murderer, right?

Just as I was about to say something to voice my concern, Becks disappeared to the right, down yet another little path.

I darted after her.

"Where are we going?" I tried to keep the panic out of my voice.

"Patience, patience," she said.

I could sense the cheeky grin on her face.

"No, seriously," I tried hard to sound calm.

"It's not far now. Just around the corner."

If she'd intended to make me feel better, she'd failed.

We were now descending along quite a steep ravine into another pit of complete darkness caused by a clump of olive trees. At one point, she stopped, and I was about to let out a sigh of relief when I realised that she was merely holding back a branch, like a doorway, so that I could get through.

I ducked past her, breaking my first resolve from earlier, and then veered off onto a rocky step to the side and waited for her to take the lead downhill again.

"It's just through here," she said and ducked, pushing another clump of branches and holding them back for me.

As I ducked past her, I stepped into a small clearing. Directly ahead of me, over the lower tree line, lay a breathtaking, shimmering, silver expanse. At first, I was baffled by its brightness after all the darkness we had just come through. Then I realised it was a large lake nestled in the surrounding hillside. It was beautiful. I struggled to look away, trying to take it all in.

I felt Becks move next to me. When I finally dragged my gaze off of the magical surroundings, I noticed Becks had fetched something from under a tree and was dragging it into the clearing. It took a while before I realised it was a camp bed.

She pulled the bed out and positioned it like a pew looking out over the lake and took a seat. She patted the space next to her. "Best seats in the house."

Not knowing what else to do, I sat down next to her.

We stayed like that, silent, looking out at the breathtaking vista in front of us for a long moment.

"Told you it would be worth it," she finally said in a low voice, as if she was not wanting to disturb the night air.

Becks picked up her backpack and started rummaging around in it.

Oh, my God! I was right. She was going for her weapon. A gun? A taser? I started searching the ground around me for anything I could grab to use in my defence. How could I have been so stupid to say yes to going on the back of a bike with a complete stranger? My heart thumped in my chest now. I tried to think back to our journey here, but the winding walk had completely disorientated me. Even if I was let loose, I would have had no idea how to get back to Eressos.

Then, I caught sight of it. Across the water, way on the other side of the enormous shimmering expanse, I noticed a small building visible only in the halo of a single outside light. The building itself showed no signs of being lived in. Could the occupants have just gone to bed? I had no idea how late it was. Or was it already closed up for the winter, like most of the houses I had seen in the village? I knew I had quite a powerful voice, and I could imagine through the quiet stillness it would carry for some distance, but would it still fall on deaf ears?

"Who…who lives there?" I asked, needing to clear my throat to sound less strangled.

"Monks, I believe."

I turned towards her, not sure if I'd heard correctly, and I caught sight of her stretching out towards me with something.

I reacted instinctively and tried to knock the object out of her hand. However, I missed, and just in time I realised it was a tumbler of some sort. Luckily, as well as unfortunately, my fumbled attempt at self-defence just looked like I had startled.

"Jeez! Jumpy much!" Becks pulled back her hand out of my way. "Let's try that again." She reached over once more, offering me the item again. "I brought some supplies. If you could stop jumping about and hold these, I can try to pour us a drink."

I swallowed hard, trying to calm my nerves, and took the tumblers from her. I realised they were metal cups with five ridges. I gently felt them in the dark and recognised them as concertina tumblers, like the ones we used to use as kids when camping. Each one comprised four telescopic rings that collapsed inside each other for compact storage. When you wanted to use them, the rings extended out like a short telescope. I always worried that I might put pressure on the top of the cup and in so doing, collapse them accidentally while full of liquid. Right now, I refused to entertain that thought. There was already too much to worry about.

Becks produced a glass hip flask from her backpack.

Despite the bright moonlight and the reflection off the water, it was still difficult to see, and I worried about how true Becks' aim would be. I tried to hold the cups out as steady as possible, hoping she could not notice them shake in the dark.

I heard, rather than saw, a short dash of liquid pouring into each cup. Suddenly, the thought occurred to me that Becks did not need a gun or a taser. She could just as easily be planning to drug me and… and… I couldn't even bring myself to contemplate what could happen next.

"Glad I brought some of the strong stuff," Becks said, returning the hip flask to her backpack. Then she took one cup from me. "Right, get that down ya." She clinked my cup. "*Yamas.*"

I sniffed the liquid. It was strong! I hesitated, waiting for Becks to take the first sip.

"Damn, that is good," she said, "even if I say so myself." Her giggle seemed to reverberate off the surrounding trees.

By that stage, the evening's events had completely frazzled my nerves, and I really needed a drink—the stronger, the better. I threw back the shot.

Instantly, the fiery liquid burnt the back of my throat, and I started to cough. Oh, my God! Had she really poisoned me? I felt the burn of the alcohol as it hit my empty stomach, followed by an almost instant warmth spreading through my chest. The taste was not entirely vile. In fact, it was quite sweet, something akin to sweet rum. It was actually not bad.

6

———————

ive shots of the warming poison later, I was feeling far more relaxed. It didn't feel as if I'd had a lot to drink, really, but I was certainly tipsier than I had been in quite some time. I reasoned it must have resulted from the combined impact of the alcohol, all the fresh air, and adrenaline. After all, being led to an unknown, dark, deserted location in the middle of nowhere by a complete stranger can probably do that to one.

To be honest, all my trepidation seemed to have miraculously disappeared or rather morphed into excited, nervous giddiness, like a teenager on a first date. How I could have registered this as a "first date", I was not sure, but obviously my unconscious was more on the ball than I was. For starters, I was convinced that Becks was straight, and other than the passing comment the other night at the party, I certainly had not registered that she had any designs on me. As far as I was concerned, I was just having a wild and unimaginable evening doing something way outside my comfort zone and, actually, if I was honest, loving the thrill of it.

However, my sense of excited euphoria evaporated instantly at the feeling of Beck's arm around my back and her hand gently stroking the nape of my neck. My first thought was that something was crawling on me and she was brushing it off, but then her touch felt soft and lingering—far too long to be assisting an errant creature. I turned to glance at her and found her bright eyes twinkling in the moonlight, staring straight at me. My mouth went dry. What was she doing?

"You are exquisite," she said matter-of-factly.

I tried to smile through my surprise, at least some small part of my brain registering that it was a compliment, while the larger part grappled for sense. "Becks, I—"

As it happened, I was saved the effort of needing to find more words. Beck's hand pulled me towards her and I realised too late that the trajectory was going to carry my lips directly to hers.

The kiss felt strange, yet exhilarating. It somehow felt different from any kiss I could remember at that moment. But, then again, it had been such a long time since I'd kissed anybody that I couldn't be quite sure whether I was merely imagining that through my tipsy haze.

Even though we were drinking the same thing, the alcohol tasted different on her lips. That intrigued me and soon I was eagerly tasting and relishing the new flavours. While I wholly focused on that, my body seemed to have a mind of its own, acting on autopilot, and before I knew it, there was an alarming welling up of desire in my gut.

To add to my alarm, my full, undivided attention was then arrested by the sensation of hands—fingers—running up the sides of my torso, sliding my T-shirt up as they went. The fingers were cool, small, but adept. They slipped underneath my bra and cupped my breast, causing my breath to catch dangerously, considering we were still in a mouth lock at that moment.

Whether it was the alcohol or the adrenaline that had pickled my brain, I didn't know. All I could register was that it, all of it, felt so good. I wanted more. I leant into her touch. She got the message and, despite my reticence to break the kiss, removed my T-shirt and my bra, pulling them over my head.

Only then, when the cool night air hit my naked body, did I falter for a moment—a brief, faint flash of indecision and disorientation.

"Brief" on account of Becks taking one of my nipples into her mouth and sucking firmly, flooding my brain with dopamine and causing my diaphragm to contract, taking in another large gulp of air. My moan sounded too loud for the environment, but I didn't care.

Before I knew it, Becks had me lying on the camp bed half-naked with her head between my legs, playing me like a mouth organ. Hoarse passion and the moaning melody of my orgasm drifted out across the lake.

When we finally left the lake, rather than taking me back to the party, Becks took me straight home to Jacko's house. That was just as well, as I later discovered that it was almost sunrise.

Who knew what Sophia, Giorgos, and the rest of the party must have thought about our disappearance. I could only hope that they had not noticed.

Outside Jacko's house, Becks pulled up and I stumbled off the back of the scooter, still a little unsteady on my feet both from the alcohol and the wake of the happy hormones that had recently been rushing through my body.

I expected Becks to drive off immediately. Instead, she parked the scooter up and got off. Before I realised what was about to happen, she grabbed hold of my hand and pulled me towards her into a long, slow kiss. Finally, she pulled away slightly and whispered, "I'll see you tomorrow."

My foggy brain was not sure whether that was a statement or a question. I also didn't know how to answer. I blinked and she must have taken that as an affirmative. The best I could do was contort my face into a silly smile before dashing into Jacko's house as quickly as I could.

7

_____

That morning, Jacko and I had arranged to have a video call. I suspected she wanted to check that I had actually gone to the Greek evening and probably needed to reassure herself that I was coping on my own without her. So, at 8:00 a.m., I hauled my severely under-slept bones out of bed, splashed some cold water over my bloodshot eyes, threw on a T-shirt and a pair of shorts and, armed with very strong coffee, propped myself up on the chair at her garden table.

Promptly, as always, at 8.30 a.m., my tablet beeped, and the screen flashed with Jacko's profile picture. I hit the answer button and, in the cheeriest, most chirpy voice that I could manage, wished her a good morning.

It didn't take Jacko long to raise a suspicious eyebrow. "Are you okay, Spice?"

Too late I realised my mistake. I needed to tone down my cheeriness, otherwise Jacko would certainly suss that something major was up.

"Yes, yes, fine. Must be all the fresh air." My mind flooded with images of the lake, the bejewelled night sky, and the fireworks in my mind that augmented my view of it as Becks did unspeakable things to me.

"So, how was it?" Jacko's voice brought me back to the present. "Did my friends do okay by you?"

I could feel my cheeks flush. Doing "okay by me" was an understatement. I dampened down the vivid memory of the extensive orgasm I had been treated to by her friend.

"Did they look after you?" she asked, sounding more suspicious and a touch worried now.

I squirmed. I was definitely not ready to reveal to Jacko any of what happened. "Yes, they did." I forced myself to sound as neutral as possible.

"I was missed, of course." Jacko's naughty grin revealed she knew she was fishing for compliments. She also knew that her frank, egotistical cheekiness was part of her charm.

I nodded. "So, when are you heading back?" I asked, trying to change the topic.

"There seems to be a hold-up with one supplier for a specialty part I need."

I still wasn't sure whether I was pleased or sad to know that there was a delay. Of course, I would have loved Jacko to be back as soon as possible, as I was there to visit her, after all. It was just that, for some reason, I wasn't ready to tell Jacko about the previous evening's escapades. At the time, I blamed fatigue and an element of aftershock.

The one thing I knew for sure was that it was a one-time occurrence. I would probably not see Becks again, unless I went to another Greek evening, which I couldn't imagine doing either, having had enough excitement to last me for some time. I would just make up an excuse next time. Jacko's house was, after all, a lovely place, with a beautiful view, and I had everything I needed right there. I could happily haul up there in the quiet, solitary bliss until Jacko's return.

When my attention returned to the conversation, Jacko was smiling quizzically at me. "Spice? Are you okay?"

I took a sip of my coffee to gain composure, but I couldn't help the smile that remained on my face.

"Do I get the feeling little Spice has had a bit of excitement?" My dear friend had always had a terribly uncanny way of knowing exactly what was going through my mind.

I considered coming clean.

Nope! I couldn't do it.

This was unfamiliar territory for Jacko and me and our friendship. Yes, she occasionally had mentioned seeing other women, but the shoe had, so far, not been on the other foot, and I certainly was not ready to slip on those Birkenstocks, especially since it involved one of her Greek circle.

I shook my head, taking care not to seem overly defensive.

"Hmm, well, either way," Jacko continued, "I'm pleased if you did. I did say you'd get the hang of island life." She laughed. "I aim to be back as soon as possible, so that I can pester you in person until you reveal all."

I knew my lovely Jacko would fulfil her promise. But for the time being, a part of me was very pleased to have a reprieve. The other enormous part of me really hoped she would hurry back. I missed my friend.

I had not put the phone down from Jacko for more than a few minutes, barely having sat back down with a second cup of coffee, when there came a shout from the other side of the garden gate. I glanced around, assessing whether I was visible and if there was somewhere to hide, but realised too late that I was in perfect eye line from the road. Thank goodness I had resisted doing some topless sunbathing.

What was more, I instantly recognised the voice hollering from the gate as the last person I wanted to see, given the crazy events of the previous evening.

Before I could answer, Becks had figured out how to open the gate from the outside and had made her way along the little path towards where I sat, frozen in a patch of sun, unable to decide whether to run or pretend I was invisible.

"Good morning." Her tone was unfairly bright and cheery. I had hoped that she would at least be suffering a little.

I grunted.

"I thought you might say that," she said, and held out a small white box of painkillers.

I held up my hand instinctively, driven by all manner of self-preservation, wanting to refuse any bright ideas this woman might have. "I'm okay, thanks. I'll just pay the penance. It is, after all, well deserved." I took a sip of my black coffee.

"Well, horses and water. Some people believe in retribution. The rest of us like to get away scot-free."

I bet she did like to get away with all sorts.

"Well, if you won't accept my medicinal offering, how about the hair of the dog?"

I looked at my watch. "It's not even ten in the morning," I said, sounding more alarmed than I had intended.

"Well, somewhere in the world, it is ten in the evening." She shrugged. "I thought I could take you to Gavathos and show you one of my favourite beaches."

The thought of getting on the back of her scooter in my current condition made me feel quite bilious. I shook my head. "Thanks, but I think I'll just recover in Greek time."

"Are all you Brits so scared of a bit of adventure?" Becks asked without a speck of malice.

I shook my head. "No, but some of us have a strong sense of self-preservation."

"Come on, it'll be great. It's a perfect day for the beach, not too hot, and I bet you have not been to Gavathos yet."

She was right. I hadn't been there, or anywhere yet, and I had been considering a day on the beach recently to get rid of my luminescent pale pallor.

"Come on, you'll love it and hand on heart,"—her actions matched her words—"I promise I won't feed you potent home brews again. Instead, I'll treat you to a picnic of tzatziki, bread, and chilled local wine, which I've packed in my cooler for us."

My stomach grumbled in response to the mention of food. I hadn't eaten since I had the taste of the hummus and pickled fish at the Greek night—probably part of the reason I felt as bad as I did.

"Wait, let me guess," she continued before I could respond, "you have a stacked diary, crammed full of people to do and places to see today."

"I don't do…" I stopped myself. The comment was not worth a response. Something in me really wanted her to know I do not make a habit of being fucked senseless by a relative stranger on a camp bed, under a full moon in the middle of the Greek countryside. Thinking of it like that made it even harder to believe that it was exactly what had happened.

She must have noticed the inevitable flush that crept up my cheeks, because she laughed her soft, bubbly laugh. "I gather something has got you a bit excited."

I felt myself blush even harder.

"Seriously," she said, "come on. It'll be fun and at least when Jacko comes back, you can tell her you did something other than mope around on her veranda in your pjs all day."

The thought of Jacko's potential disappointment in me for moping around while she wasn't around to play tour guide pushed a button. What did I have to lose?

"Okay," I finally said. "But no more funny business. I'm not like that!" The moment I said it, I realised how potentially insulting it was.

"Not like that, huh?" Her tone was guarded. "Like what exactly? You mean like me? Friendly, generous, considerate? Happy to show newbies new and exciting places." She paused.

I squirmed. "I'm sorry. I didn't mean it like that."

By now my face was burning red hot. I wished so hard I could take my comment back. I didn't want to upset her. After all, I did like her, and she was clearly kind and friendly—perhaps a bit too friendly if she did this with every new person in town—and it was me who had given in to her advances. In fact, I had begged her for more when she started to kiss and touch me. Oh, God! I cringed as more memories flooded back.

"Well, if it is that, I'm pleased to say I enjoyed it, too," she said and winked.

A wave of relief combined with something akin to terror washed over me. At least I hadn't offended her.

"I promise I'll not take advantage of you again," she held up her hand in a scout's salute, "without your prior consent." She winked again.

"It's not—"

"Come on, get your kit. Let's go. I'll wait here. You have fifteen minutes to get ready. That should be plenty of time. Or are you one of those 'got to do my hair' types?"

I shook my head and without consciously deciding to do so, I got up and headed indoors.

8

_I_f the results of the previous evening were anything to go by, I had become a new firm believer in the fact that adrenaline skyrocketed, no pun intended, arousal. And if Becks was intending to push me to new heights with the journey to the beach, she was certainly going about it the right way.

The road to Gavathos, with its many blind hairpin bends and barrier-free sides, was one of the scariest I had ever come across. That, added to my already crippling anxiety levels about sitting on the back of an open moving vehicle over which I had no control made me cling to her waist with white knuckles. I only forced myself to loosen my grip when it occurred to me that I might be restricting her airflow.

She, however, did not seem to mind.

Finally, after a few more twists and turns through a mostly deserted village, we reached the low plateau near the coast. Becks pulled up to the side. We were again seemingly in the middle of nowhere.

"Right, we're here."

"Where exactly is here?" I asked, unable to make out any particular defining features. I recalled passing a few signs on our way there, but since I couldn't read Greek, they didn't help much.

"Is this Gavathos?"

She shook her head. "Not quite. We're not far from there, at Kampos Beach."

I nodded as if that explained everything perfectly.

She parked up the bike and grabbed the bags she'd been supporting between her legs in the footwell.

Like a stray puppy, exceedingly out of my depth again, I followed her down a hidden path into the sand dunes. Within a few minutes, we emerged on a spectacular, long and narrow stretch of beach. The first thing that struck me was how rough the sea was—not stormy, exactly, but there were far more waves than I had seen so far in Skala Eressos.

"I come here quite often if I want to get away from the crowds in Eressos and I want to have a fun swim," Becks said.

I nodded.

"The sea is a bit rougher, but more importantly, it's warmer, which towards the edge of the season can be nice."

I stood around admiring the scenery while she started to lay out a sun-shield that consisted of a large square lycra-like sheet, secured in each corner by a bag of sand and then propped up by two poles. As soon as that was erected, she lay out her sarong and I joined her by laying out my towel.

"Shall we swim first?" she asked.

By now I was quite hungry, but I decided it was better to follow her lead.

I had dressed conservatively in shorts and a T-shirt over my bikini. I knew a lot of the women in Skala Eressos preferred to swim naked. This was a "secluded beach", so there was a high likelihood that naked swimming would be possible. Although most boundaries of modesty between us had already been well and truly shattered the night before, it had taken place under the cover of darkness, not to mention the thick haze of alcohol. Right then, the sun was shining far too bright and, thanks to the ride there, I had sobered up completely.

For Becks, none of these complications seemed to be a problem. With a few smooth movements, she stripped off and headed towards the sea.

I tried not to stare. She had a beautiful body.

I realised that I hadn't actually seen her naked, and I cringed at the realisation that I had been a proverbial pillow princess the previous night—allowing her to do all the pleasuring, while I lay back and drowned in the stars, both real and orgasmic.

At the water's edge, she turned as if she could feel my eyes on the back of her, to give me a full-frontal view of her beautiful breasts, ripped abs and neatly coiffured triangle. Oh, my God, she was in great shape!

I waited until she had gone all the way into the sea and seemed preoccupied with diving under the waves before I quickly stripped off and trotted after her.

The water's edge, like in Skala Eressos, was encrusted with sharp pebbles, so I had to slow down to traverse the abrasive surface. I prayed she wouldn't turn back at that moment to witness me inelegantly wincing and wobbling my way in.

Despite her assurances to the contrary, the water was bracing. It was not quite as bad as Skala Eressos, but cold enough to stop my breath and obliterate all possibility of silently, with aplomb, easing myself into the surf.

After a few deep inhalations, I managed to advance as far as my belly button before she turned to look at me. She was probably wondering what was taking so long.

I gave myself a stern pep-talk and dived forward under an oncoming wave.

After the initial "fuck-me-my-heart-is-about-to-stop" and "my-lungs-are-going-to-freeze-over" moments, it felt fantastic—euphoric almost—similar to, I imagined, a near-death experience. I guess there were a few similarities.

I joined her and we frolicked about, diving under waves and allowing the more transparent, almost crystal-clear waves to crash over us. I couldn't help grinning like a Cheshire cat. If only Lewis Caroll had met the cats in Greece. It was fun. It was more than fun. I was *having* fun. There was something compulsive and inherently exuberant about the simple activity of jumping through waves. Again, I wondered how much my spiked adrenaline levels had to do with my euphoria.

"Come on," she said, waving me deeper. "There's a sandbank just over there." She ducked under the next wave and started swimming out further.

Again, I followed.

When I reached her, I tried to stand, and I realised the seabed had transitioned from chest deep to a depth barely above the knees. The waves were bigger there on account of the shallowness. I had assumed she meant for us to stop there, but again I was wrong. I followed her as she continued to jump through the waves and head out even farther.

Finally, she stopped and turned, beckoning to me. "It's calmer here."

She was right. A few more strokes beyond the sandbank, we were beyond the break. It was deeper and there was a nice steady swell. I turned over onto my back and floated, allowing my body to bob in the undulating waves. I took a deep breath and tried to remember when I had last actually had a beach holiday.

Just then, I felt something crawl around my back and legs. I shrieked and opened my eyes to look straight into Becks' cheeky grin a few inches away from me. She had swum up to me and wrapped her arms around my back and under my knees, cradling me like a baby. I wanted to squirm and pull away, but I didn't dare.

"Relax," she said decisively.

I could feel her bare breasts pressed into my side as she took me more firmly in her arms.

The warmth of her body soaked into my skin, and her hard nipples pressed into me. The idea stopped me short.

God, it didn't take much these days.

I allowed her to take hold of me gently and guide me over the waves. She swung me around in a circle. For some reason, this made us both giggle.

I allowed my arm to rest on her shoulders. This pulled us closer. I realised what she was about to do only a fraction of a second too late as she brought her head down and took my nipple into her warm mouth. The sucking sensation on my already sensitive nipple, a leftover from the night before, pulled at my core and I felt myself unfurl like a flower in the morning sunlight. In an instant, a wildfire of desire blazed a trail from my nipple across the rest of my body.

Sensing the effect she had on me, she let my legs go, allowing them to sink. Now facing each other, she kissed me and pulled me even closer to her. I felt like I was feeding off her warmth as I devoured her salty lips. I could think of nothing but satisfying my desire.

Moments later, she pulled away and winked. "Someone seems a little hungry," she said. "Shall we get out and have some lunch?"

I could feel the flush creep over my cheeks, even in the cold sea. Before I could think of a witty response, she'd already turned and started back to shore.

After the bracing excitement in the sea, I needed a little distance and warmth to recover my composure. I laid my towel down a short distance away from the sunshade.

"There is plenty of room under here," Becks said.

"Just wanting to warm up a bit."

"I thought that was quite hot." Becks grinned at me.

Words failed me again. I lay down on my back, propped on my elbows. I closed my eyes and enjoyed the sun's warmth seeping into my skin. I leant my head back and focussed on my breathing and tried to clear my mind like my yoga instructor had taught. Unfortunately, I was acutely aware that Becks was only a few feet away, scratching around in her bag. I thought she might be putting out the picnic things, but when I peeped over, she was nowhere near the cool-bag. I closed my eyes again and tried to breathe from my diaphragm.

Then, I heard an odd sound. It was the distinct clutter of a camera shutter releasing.

Shit!

The recent trauma from Rory "the Rottweiler" from the *Daily Mail*, who had for some reason developed an unnatural fixation on me, came rushing back. After I did an innocuous little interview about the lesser-known spice trade, he had somehow become obsessed with me and began stalking me. It took twelve months and a court order to get him to stop popping up in hotels and pointing his camera in my direction on street corners.

Oh, he'd love catching me on a beach naked! I could see his headline now: "Ex-spice queen branches out into spice of a different kind."

I snapped open my eyes.

Instead of a lurking Rory, I was relieved to see just the two of us still there. It took me a few seconds to identify the source of the shutter. Then I saw it. Becks was holding up a very expensive-looking SLR camera, pointing it at me, snapping and rotating it from portrait to landscape and back to portrait.

"What are you doing?" A sense of panic and betrayal rose in me like a volcano. Was she a spy? A secret reporter? Was this all a set-up?

She lowered the camera and I could see her broad grin. "Just taking a few pics." She obviously registered my alarm and her grin faded. "Surely, you don't mind."

"Actually, I do. Who the fuck are you working for? Who sent you?" I sat up and pulled the towel up around me. "I should have known." I got up and started to gather my things, feeling the need to get out of there as quickly as possible.

"Wait," Becks said.

I had started stuffing my clothes into my bag when I felt her cool fingers' grip around my wrists.

I looked up and saw the look of concern on her face. "Hey, what's going on?" she asked.

"Usually, people ask before they take pictures of me. And certainly not when I'm naked." Even I was a little surprised by the anger in my own voice. "Which newspaper are you with? Who are you working for? Was this the plan all along? Or is this how you make your money or get your kicks?"

She shook her head and I could see the serious look of alarm in her eyes. "No. No. I'm not working for anyone. I'm not a reporter."

She faltered, and I thought, here we go. Not so smooth now, getting caught in her own lies.

"You have to believe me. I'm just me. Yes, I'm a photographer. That's what I do. But I am not taking photos *for* anyone. They're just for me."

Her tone stopped me. She sounded so sincere. I did not know what to make of this. Could she be lying? I probably wouldn't have believed her if she hadn't looked so utterly shocked.

"Honestly." She let go of one of my wrists and crossed her heart with a finger. "As I said, I am not a reporter. I'm a leisure photographer by trade. You looked so beautiful lying there in the sun, and very rarely do I get to capture such beautiful subjects. I really didn't think you'd mind. I'm so very sorry. I should have asked." She waited for me to respond. "Honestly, I'm sorry."

I scoffed but suddenly felt unsure whether I was still angry or flattered. I felt myself relax and allowed her to pull me towards her.

She kissed me chastely. "I really do apologise" she whispered, "for not asking you first." She kissed me again and then pulled back a little. "But I'm not sorry for wanting to take your picture." Her dimples returned. "You truly are beautiful and I'd very much like to capture you."

It was impossible to stay angry with those dimples.

"Please, may I," she said, more quietly.

I didn't know what to say.

"I tell you what. If you let me capture you, and at the end of the day you still feel uncomfortable, you can have the film."

My ears pricked up at the word "film".

"Film?"

She nodded. "The pros still use film, believe it or not." She met my gaze straight on. "What do you say?"

I felt myself capitulate. "I will hold you to that." As I said that, I was a little embarrassed by how easily she had swayed me.

She nodded and lifted a hand in a scout salute. "I promise."

She took my hand and guided me back to the place where I had been lying in the sun and urged me to lie back on my towel. She retreated to her sarong where she had rested her camera. She smiled such a sweet, reassuring smile that any remnants of my ire from earlier melted like ice cream in the sand.

"What do you want me to do?" I asked, feeling very self-conscious.

"Just do what you were doing. Relax and enjoy the sunshine."

I lay back and closed my eyes, trying to dampen down the uncomfortable squirming sensation that was building inside me. I heard the shutter release once, then twice, then it resumed the slow almost hypnotic, rhythmic pattern. Without needing to look, I became aware that Becks was moving around me, circling me, covering different angles, I presumed. My self-consciousness was beginning to bubble uncontrollably inside me.

As if she could sense that, I heard her voice, soft and reassuring. "That's right. Feel the relaxation…the warmth." She continued to click, click, click.

"Sit up," she said.

I opened my eyes a little surprised by her sudden request.

"Sit up, with your hands behind you, supporting you."

I did as I had been asked.

"That's it. Now, lean your head back. Drop your right knee and raise your left. Bring your foot up towards your right knee. Now, imagine you are being kissed all over by the sun…by an attentive lover. Imagine them whispering in your ear. It tickles…. They are nuzzling your neck with rough tongue kisses."

I smiled, feeling self-conscious, but I leant my head back, exposing my neck to the imaginary kisses.

What started off as her directed instructions, soon turned into my vivid imaginings. I could feel the lips. I could feel the caresses. And I wanted more.

I lay back and with gentle fingers followed the path that she had described the lips were trailing down from my neck along my upper body. When it came to my nipples, I felt them contract. I imagined my finger was a powerful tongue flicking one gently and sucking at it. I briefly pinched my puckered, tender flesh causing myself to gasp. The imaginary kisses continued down over my belly, circling my belly button. I knew by now I was wet.

I was so engrossed in my reverie, I had not realised the cluttering shutter had stopped. I felt a tickle on my torso. Becks had come over and was leaning down over me, her hair dragging on my skin. And, as if she could read my mind, she flicked my nipple with her tongue and then sucked it into her mouth.

I suddenly felt self-conscious. I tried to sit up.

With a firm hand on my chest, she pushed me down to lay back on the towel while another hand trailed along the inside of my thigh from my knee up towards my centre. She gently caressed the far nipple while her teeth and tongue continued to tease the one closest to her. I suddenly felt her cool fingers touch and begin to gently caress my most intimate lips. Then, she opened me up and ran her fingers along my soft, by now dripping, inner folds.

"Oh, God," I hissed.

Rather than penetrating me as I had hoped, she caressed that most sensitive part of my inner folds, sliding her fingers from my clitoris down and up, connecting perfectly with my pulsing nerves. She insisted on teasing and cajoling and dragging every ounce of pleasure out of me. I felt like I was about to burst. The perfectly timed nip and suck on my nipples yanked me even further. I spread my legs wide. I ached to feel her inside me. She slipped one, then two drenched fingers inside me. With rhythmic, deft strokes inside and out, she coaxed my desire further. It felt like every tendril of my awareness was being gathered and drawn to the tips of her incessant fingers. I forgot to breathe. I was sure even my heart would stop, but I didn't care. I could think and feel nothing else other than the tips of her fingers exquisitely coaxing, tuning, and ramping up my desire into an intense, condensed singularity.

Then, when I could not stand it anymore, and I was ready to surrender and meet my maker, she plunged deep inside me, hitting my most intimate sweet spot while simultaneously biting down on my nipple. The shock and intensity of the sensations set off a veritable cosmic event in my being. I exploded like a supernova, sending stratospheric shockwaves into the universe.

I lay there recovering until, finally, I became aware of her stirring. I opened my eyes.

She was sitting next to me, grinning and looking inordinately pleased with herself. "You are beautiful," she said. "Thank you."

Right then, I had the weirdest sensation, the weirdest most incongruous thought: Here was a beautiful, attractive woman, who had just given me yet another, probably the most mind-blowing, orgasm I'd had in quite some time, and yet I felt nothing other than admiration, maybe a mild sense of affection for her.

I could easily fuck her. In fact, I really hoped to have an opportunity to give her even a fraction of the pleasure she had just given me. However my heart seemed to remain unmoved. Yes, the sex was great. The frisson was exhilarating. But somehow, it seemed empty. Perhaps this was still far too early to expect myself to suddenly have fallen. However, that was what I really craved more than anything.

Whether it was my silence that broke the spell, or if she could somehow read my thoughts, I would not know. She sat up and moved away, going back to her bag under the sunshade.

"Would you like some water?"

The question seemed strangely surreal under the circumstances.

I nodded, and she produced a large frozen two-litre bottle of water. I took a long, thirsty drink. I hadn't realised how thirsty I was. Somehow in my eagerness, I allowed some water to escape from my mouth and dribbled down my chin onto my chest. Before I knew it, she had picked up a camera and was snapping away again.

"Enough, already. If you carry on like this, you'll kill me."

She giggled. "True, I should probably feed you first."

I laughed. "Yes, please."

I watched as she laid out the picnic feast she had promised.

Later that afternoon, once the heat had grown a little too intense for both of us, she took me back to Eressos. She had a dusk shoot. A honeymoon couple wanted photos of them at the chapel at sunset.

She kissed me goodbye. It was a nice kiss.

She was about to get back on her scooter.

"Have you not forgotten something?" I asked, quickly.

She looked puzzled.

I stretched out my hand and wiggled by fingers. "The film."

She rolled her eyes. "I hoped you'd forgotten." She beamed me one of her mischievous grins.

I smiled. "Never."

She reached into the front pocket of her backpack and took out the small back cylinder. "Pity," she said. "I would have enjoyed developing those."

She leaned into me again and kissed me.

I took the cylinder.

She got on her bike, and I watched her disappear down the road. Once again, I marvelled at the apparent inertia of my feelings. She seemed to be "a good woman" as my aunt used to say. I found her funny, charming, sweet, and certainly sexy. Yes, she could arouse me in a matter of seconds, yet my heart remained unmoved. Had I somehow lost the ability to love? Had my years focussing on business finally, literally, turned me into a proverbial "stone butch?"

9

I had managed to hibernate and keep out of trouble for almost two weeks since my last outing with Becks. I had not seen her around. She had told me she would be busy with back-to-back shoots for a few days, since the major holiday resort in Skala Eressos had received a large off-season bird-watching tour group. This suited me perfectly. I really needed to put a stop to whatever was happening between her and me. It was not what I really wanted, and I certainly did not want to mislead her. I was hoping to have a coffee with her to explain and clear the air before Jacko returned. However, that was not to be, as for some reason, we had not exchanged telephone numbers.

In any event, Jacko had texted to say she would be arriving via ferry on that Friday at midday.

I took her car to the port in Mytilene to fetch her. The control freak in Jacko would not allow me to drive her back, even though she had hardly slept a wink during the night on the ferry.

We arrived home in the late afternoon.

The only recovery time she required was to take a shower and change into fresh clothes. Then, she joined me on her terrace, armed with two cold bottles of beer.

I was genuinely interested in hearing about her time with the Russian Count and I really tried to concentrate and get absorbed by the intricacies of violin maintenance, but my mind had a will of its own. It kept whirling in a loop of trepidation about how I was going to break the news about Becks to Jacko. I knew Becks was one of her friends. Or, if I was lucky, merely an acquaintance. Still though, it somehow felt strange to have had such an intimate encounter—encounters even—with someone Jacko knew.

Jacko's phone rang. I jumped. Clearly, my nerves were on edge.

Jacko gave me a strange, brief look, but answered the phone.

It was Giorgos. He had heard Jacko was back and phoned to invite us to join a group of them at Portokali, a small bar on the edge of the main square in the village, later that evening. Apparently, his niece, Thalia, a singer-songwriter, was performing with a band of local musicians. Secretly, I had hoped Jacko would be too tired and we could retire to bed early. I was not quite ready to face the outside world yet. At least with live music, it would be more difficult to talk about deep things. Then, a horrid thought struck: God forbid Becks would be there, too!

Unfortunately, Jacko had more energy than a dynamo on speed and after a mere glance in my direction, I saw her nod and accept the invitation.

***

We arrived at Portokali a little late, about three-quarters of the way through Thalia's first set. By then, all the seats were taken, leaving standing room around the edges only. It didn't particularly bother me except that standing around felt a little awkward when you didn't know anybody. I would have preferred to take a quiet seat in the corner somewhere and fade into the background.

Jacko had disappeared into the bar to get us a drink.

I hastily scanned the crowd to see if I could spot Becks. The outside of the bar was not very well lit, but to my relief, the coast seemed clear.

Jacko finally reappeared at the door to the bar with our drinks. I could see her try to figure out a way to get back to me. More people had arrived, and she eventually seemed to give up, leaning against the door, presumably until the end of the set.

After another song or two, the young Thalia stopped and said something in Greek, to which the audience erupted in excited applause and whoops. I saw Jacko step aside out of the doorway just in time to avoid being carried back in to the building by the mass rampage towards the bar.

Eventually, Jacko zigzagged her way back to where I had found a little eddy from the crowd.

"Better late than never. Cheers," she said, and handed me an ice-cold bottle of beer.

A storm was moving in and the temperatures had dropped. A shiver ran through my body at the feel of the cold bottle on such a chilled night. Perhaps I should have opted for a hot chocolate.

"So now for the moment of truth," Jacko said, turning her attention squarely on me. "Tell me, who is the lucky lady?"

I frowned and tried to look blank as convincingly as possible.

"Come on," she said, gently bumping her shoulder against mine. "It's me. Don't pretend you don't know what I mean."

I raised my eyebrows. Just then, my eye caught the familiar silhouette of the blonde ponytail and a prickle of tension crawled over my skin. Of course, Jacko noticed my distraction and turned to see what I had seen. Becks also saw us grinned, waved and, to my great trepidation, made her way over.

"Hey," Jacko embraced Becks in a warm hug. They exchanged niceties, Becks welcoming her back from her work trip.

"You arrived just in time," Jacko said. Still with her arm around Becks' shoulders, she coaxed her into the huddle.

"Have you two met? This is—"

"Becks. Yes, we have," I blurted, and extended my hand in a formal handshake.

Becks hesitated for a split second and a frown flashed across her features. Luckily, she played along. She took my hand and smiled.

I worried Jacko would notice the weirdness. So, I continued quickly. "Yes, we met the night you took me to the first Greek evening."

Becks nodded. "Yes, at the Greek evening." She hesitated again. "It's nice to see you again, Terry." She winked.

I squirmed.

"Well, you arrived just in time." Jacko continued. "Spice here was just going to tell us about the mystery lady she met while I was away."

I gave Jacko a scowl and shook my head, wishing the earth would swallow me whole.

"Oh, really? How exciting! Oh, please, do tell," Becks said, holding my gaze.

"A lady doesn't kiss and tell," I said, trying to front it out.

"Nothing lady-like about you. I have known Spice a long time and not seen her colour like that," Jacko said.

It was true, I could feel the patches of red appear around my ears and neck.

"I hope they gave you a good time," Becks said, a dimple forming on her cheek.

Not a moment too soon, a loud thudding noise interrupted us as Thalia tapped the microphone. "Ladies and gentlemen, if you could take your seats again."

The audience scurried to their chairs.

Saved by the belle. I took a sip of my drink and tried to calm down.

"Don't worry, we'll continue this later." Jacko's voice echoed in my ear in a low, deep whisper.

I choked into my drink. Jacko never made empty promises.

Meanwhile, I was excruciatingly aware of Becks, who had turned to watch the music but positioned herself exceedingly close in front of me. So close that I could smell the heady aroma of her shampoo mixed with her coconut body lotion—strong and distinctive, evoking vivid memories of our time together.

I thanked my grandmother's saints in heaven to see that Jacko's attention was on Thalia.

However, my relief was short-lived. A few minutes later, Jacko turned to Becks, and they seemed to engage in soft conversation—too soft for me to hear. This continued for most of the second half of the performance. All I could do was send up silent prayers to those saints that Becks would not reveal our secret.

Just when I was about to feign a headache as an excuse to leave and get myself out of that tense situation, Becks turned around and in an overtly formal gesture mirroring mine from earlier, held out a hand and said in a voice loud enough for Jacko to hear, "Well, it was lovely to see you again, Terry. I unfortunately have to leave, as I have an early morning shoot on the beach." She winked.

"Really?" I struggled to swallow as memories of our photoshoot flashed through my mind. "That's nice." Again, I could feel the colour creep over my cheeks. Was I old enough to pretend I was having a menopausal hot flash?

"A newlywed couple from London are heading up the Sappho's head to see the sunrise in the morning and they want a photographer to capture the moment."

I nodded, wondering which moment she meant.

Becks squeezed my hand. I let go quickly.

"Come, I'll walk you to your bike," Jacko said.

Becks nodded, and I watched with a growing sense of panic as the two of them headed out towards the square.

Jacko returned about ten minutes later. I dreaded to think what they had talked about. Jacko's demeanour hadn't changed during that time and I prayed that meant that Becks had kept her mouth shut.

By the time Thalia's final set had finished, a strong wind had come up and was buffeting everything it could reach in the square. Luckily, Portokali was sheltered by the surrounding buildings, so we did not feel the full force of the rising storm until we stepped out to head home. The brisk walk to Jacko's house was quite unpleasant. In fact, by the time we got home, both Jacko and I were so cold that Jacko offered to make us a fire.

While Jacko stoked the fire, I, at Jacko's insistence, opened another bottle of wine and poured us each a glass.

Huddled on the couch, eagerly awaiting the warm glow of the fire and a relaxed soporific nightcap before bed.

Jacko had other ideas.

After she had satisfied herself that the fire would take nicely, she jumped up and headed over to her vintage Pioneer sound system. Jacko didn't bother much with possessions, but she was the very proud owner of an extensive vinyl collection. How she got them all transported to the island when she moved here was a mystery. Within a few minutes, the sultry tones of Suzanne Vega filled the room.

Before I could protest, Jacko grabbed my hand, deftly removing the wine glass from my hand, and pulled me up off the couch.

So started the next part of the evening, with Jacko playing DJ, intermittently changing the records, taking us on a nostalgic tour of the music of our late teens and early twenties.

In between dances, Jacko and I shared intimate reminiscences—stories of our various romantic and sometimes comedic and embarrassing adventures of the heart from, in my case, our distant past.

I still could not bring myself to divulge the events of the recent few days.

At some point, well into the second bottle of wine, the opening rhythmic bars of "I'm the Only One" by Melissa Etheridge filled the room. As before, Jacko pulled me up off the couch.

In our inebriated state, the attempted, slightly too-fast two-step Jacko was trying to wrangle me into was not working very well. In the end, we just stood, me in Jacko's arms, swaying to the rhythm of the music.

Suddenly, I noticed how close we were again, like that dance we'd had at the Greek night. Every point of contact, from toes to knees to thighs, to the gentle caress of my breast against her chest, seemed to buzz with electric sensation. I could feel Jacko's powerful arms around my back, holding me close, her breath gently tickling my ear. I flashed back to the photo shoot on the beach and I imagined it was Jacko there with me, whispering into my ear, nuzzling my neck, and trailing light, sensual kisses down my body.

I closed my eyes against the exquisite onslaught in my mind.

I felt Jacko stop swaying. I snapped open my eyes, afraid that I had somehow given myself away.

What I found surprised me more. Jacko stood looking down at me. Her expression, so tender yet intense, like she was searching for my soul. I'd heard the expression of time standing still. That was it.

Whether it was thanks to the alcohol or just a culmination of an intensely emotional evening, I will never know. I felt myself lean forward and press my lips on hers. When she didn't pull away and I felt her lips part, I dived straight in, accepting the unspoken invitation.

Before I had time to consider what was happening, Jacko picked me up and carried me over to the couch in front of the roaring fire. Here she laid me down and swiftly relieved me of most of my clothes. I watched her kneel before me. One of her slightly rough, artisan hands enveloped my breast, and I felt her other hand nudging my upper thighs apart.

I held my breath. Was this actually happening? I had wanted nothing more, ever in my life. I realised in that moment I had yearned for this since the day we'd met. But nothing could have prepared me for the reality.

Her fingers filled me one at a time in strong, definite movements and her thumb stroked against my clit. I sought out her eyes and drank in her stare as she reached inside me, right the way into my soul, into the depths of my heart.

When I climaxed, far too soon, I clutched onto Jacko like I was hanging onto life itself, riding out every exquisite tremor as if it would be my last. The moment she withdrew from me, my body ached for her like an addict desperate for another fix. My fix was Jacko. How could it have taken me this long to accept the inevitable?

I was expecting us to curl on the couch and drift into a delirious post coital sleep.

I should have known that would not have been enough for Jacko. Nothing ever seemed just enough for Jacko. She was born with an insatiable hunger, and that was one of the things I so loved about her.

She got up, pulled me up and dragged me towards her bedroom.

That night, Jacko pleasured me in ways I could only have dreamt of, as I did her. We seemed to be so in tune, so natural, somehow knowing each other's bodies and desires as if they were our own. We did finally collapse, arms and legs entwined out of sheer exhaustion, and fell into a deep, peaceful sleep.

10

---

*A*s I came to, the light had filled Jacko's room already. I realised it must have been quite late.

I felt Jacko climb over me to get up. Her bed was pushed up against the wall. Halfway over she stopped and pecked me on my forehead. The gesture was light and too fleeting for my liking. I was not sure what I'd expected. Perhaps she didn't want to wake me. I pretended to still be asleep, but through slitted eyes, I watched her pad out the room. I realised she was headed downstairs to the kitchen. A few moments later, I heard the familiar sounds of the coffee pot being filled and placed on the stove.

I rolled over. Oh, my God! It had happened! I had to bite my lip to stop the euphoric giggles from bubbling out of me. It had been the night of my dreams. Jacko was finally mine. I felt myself being pulled into the mind-blowing memories of the night before.

No wait! Now was not the time to reminisce. Jacko was waiting downstairs. It was time to grab the present.

I envisioned us sitting together on her terrace in the sunshine having coffee, me taking her hand and finally having the courage to tell her how I really felt about her—how I had only just realised that I had been in love with her for years, perhaps from the very beginning, that day in the toilet cubicle.

I imagined her taking my hand and looking at me in the same way she had last night on the dance floor before we kissed, and then wrapping her powerful arms around me and kissing me more deeply. Most probably, we would end up back in bed, where we would remain until hunger and thirst forced us out at some distant future time. I felt quite giddy at the thought.

Life could not get any better.

I sat up, my cheeks aching from the smile I had plastered over my face. I'd better get to it then. Jacko was probably wondering when I'd come down.

Oh, what to wear?

I noticed Jacko's robe hanging on the wardrobe door. That would do, especially if we were going to be heading back to bed in a little while. Besides, it seemed fitting. I always wanted to be in a relationship where we wore each other's clothes. It was so sexy. If it had been one of Jacko's check shirts, I would even have worn that. It was a thing girlfriends did in the movies. That thought stopped me short. Is that what we were now, girlfriends? I felt almost jittery with joy.

When I got there, the kitchen was empty. I found Jacko sitting outside at her garden table on the terrace. The rain had stopped and the world looked shiny and damp. The thick grey cloud cover had not dissipated and there was no sign of sunshine, but I didn't mind. My mood was light and bright enough for ten suns.

I was a little disappointed to see she had found a pair of shorts and a T-shirt to wear. I had hoped she would still be in a half state of undress. *Never mind. I'll just have to think of creative ways to take them off again.*

When she saw me, she smiled, but her eyes did not quite meet mine. That should have given me a hint, but I was too preoccupied with my own jubilation.

How to start?

I noticed the pot of coffee and the second mug. I poured the oily dark liquid into the mug and sat down. I took a large sip. It was funny how even the bitterness of black coffee tasted so much better when one was blissed out.

I finally put the mug down on the table. "Jacko, I think we need to talk," I began enthusiastically.

"Yes," she said and nodded, putting her mug down, too. "I'm really sorry."

I shook my head, assuming she was referring to something trivial, like not waiting for me to have coffee. The last thing I wanted was for her to feel sorry about anything. She had made my wildest dreams come true.

Jacko continued to nod and raised her hand, stopping me short.

"No, Spice, really, let me finish."

I bit my lip, deciding it would only be fair to let her talk first.

"I really am very sorry about last night. It was a mistake. It should not have happened."

"Mistake?" The world around me fell silent. Time instantly stood still—not in a good way this time. All I could hear was the blood rushing through my ears. What? My foggy, hungover brain grappled in confusion. "What do you mean?"

"Last night was a big mistake. We should never have... you know."

She could not even bring herself to say the words.

"I'm really sorry. I really don't want my libido to ruin such a beautiful and precious friendship as we have. I hope you will forgive me. Do you think you can?"

With each word that Jacko uttered, my heart crumbled a little more.

"I mean, I don't know what came over me. We're such good friends and have been for such a long time. I would have thought that the fact that you're practically my sister would have stopped me last night."

"Sister?"

"The only thing I can think is that the wine was far more potent than I realised. I mean, man, it should have been like fucking my sister, right?" Jacko continued, clearly oblivious to what was happening for me. "You'd think that would have stopped me—"

"Fucking your sister?"

She nodded.

Words, language, failed me. I suddenly felt a strong, warm hand take hold of mine where it lay now, lifeless, on the table. I realise that Jacko had reached out and was now holding my hand. Her touch burned my skin.

"Spice, please, can you forgive me? Do you think we can put this behind us, as if it never happened?" The genuine, remorseful look in her eye shredded the last pieces of my heart.

"Behind us." I managed to say. I must have nodded because it seemed my response appeased Jacko.

"Good." She smiled. Her relief was palpable. "Good, good, good." She nodded profusely. "I'm so relieved. Thank you, Spice." She clasped her hand to her heart. "I promise nothing like that will ever happen again. I'm really sorry."

I couldn't hold myself together a minute longer. I nodded and pointed towards the inside of the house. "I'm just going…" I got up and fled.

I didn't know where to go. All I knew was that I had to get away from her. I needed to be somewhere where Jacko could not see me. Her eyes could not witness my broken heart.

On autopilot, I locked myself in the tiny bathroom. I ran the shower, not because I intended to get clean. If only I could rinse away all the pain and grief I was feeling. I prayed the sound of the running water would mask the sounds of my sobs.

In the end, I did get into the cold shower. I hoped that the stinging tendrils of the icy water would somehow distract me from the pain in my chest. At least I could use the excuse of soap in my eye to explain the red rings.

When I finally went outside again, I found Jacko busily clearing up smashed apricots from the ground where the storm had ripped them from their branches and pummelled them to the floor. I silently identified with their annihilation.

"Hey," Jacko said, smiling when she saw me. "These are such a waste."

I nodded.

"I hope the worst of the storm has passed," she said, looking up at the darkening clouds.

It was clear that, for Jacko, we were back to business as usual.

"Oh, and Beers rang," she continued. "I invited her for a hot dinner later. It would be good if you got to know her a little and maybe you can help me figure her out. You're much better at that sort of thing than I am. Maybe you can tell whether I have any hope at all." She chuckled.

The memory of Beers, the woman Jacko had said she was interested in, rushed back.

Great! That was all I needed, to spend an evening not only with Jacko in the wake of probably the most devastating moment in my life, but also facing the person who has everything I want—everything I ever wanted.

I was desperate for an excuse, any excuse, as to why I could not be around that evening. I even considered contacting Becks. Maybe I could drown myself in some rebound sex. I knew that technically, "rebound sex" was reserved for the end of a relationship. But that felt fitting. Even though Jacko and I had merely had one night together—a one-night stand—it felt like I had gained and then lost my life partner all in that same night.

I couldn't bring myself to make excuses to Jacko. She probably would not believe me, anyway. That would just remind her about my mystery woman and I was not up to being cross-questioned on top of everything.

11

J spent most of the afternoon in my room pretending to
nap. The house was quite big and the walls very thick, but
I was still acutely aware of Jacko bustling about the house. Luckily,
she respected my time-out and left me to myself. I guess she thought I
was finally following her advice about getting some R&R. She used to
tell me off regularly on our video sessions for not making enough
time to rest and relax.

The grey sky had darkened almost completely when I finally
surfaced from my room. I had figured that I couldn't really hide away
for the entire evening, too, especially since we were about to have a
visitor. To be honest, I was also a little curious to find out more about
this mystery Beers person. I hadn't even met her, and I already
hated her.

When I came into the living room, the house seemed empty. At
first, I suspected Jacko might still be outside tending to her garden.
However, when I heard the distinct sounds of water running through
the pipes, I realised she was in the shower.

I went to the fridge to get something to drink. If I was going to get
through the night, I needed a head start. It surprised me to find the

fridge filled with pre-prepared food fit for a feast. Several very good, imported bottles of wine were chilling in the door. I grabbed the open bottle of local, cheap wine we had started the previous night and poured myself a healthy glass.

I considered going to sit outside to get some fresh air but more storm clouds had gathered. It was going to be a wet night and so I decided to make myself comfortable on the couch with my legs curled up underneath me and checked my phone messages.

Since I had sold the business, the influx of messages into my inbox seemed to have dried up. People that needed me daily and could not wait for me to wake up, or even have a comfort break, now no longer even contacted me. I guessed that was life when you stepped off the treadmill. This was when you discovered who your real friends were.

My attention was dragged away from my phone to the outside when I heard someone calling out. I realised they were coming up the garden path. Two seconds later, there was a knock at the door. I glanced in the direction of the bathroom, hoping Jacko would appear, so she could deal with her guest. The shower had turned off, but there was no sign of her emerging.

I checked my watch. It was half-past six. It was a little early for dinner in Greek time, so perhaps it was just a neighbour calling.

I got up and went to see who it was. When I pulled open the door and saw who was standing on the doorstep, I froze. I blinked, horrified. Before me stood Becks.

"What are you doing here?" I said, my panic overshadowing my manners.

She was relatively smartly dressed in jeans and a low-cut, long-sleeve top—not her usual, casual look. I guessed she was going out somewhere, which also would account for the bottle of wine in her hand.

"Now is not a good time!" I hissed, praying Jacko was still happily wallowing under the hot shower.

She laughed. I couldn't understand what was funny.

"Becks, you can't be here. We're expecting guests."

Confidently, she pushed past me and entered the house. Then, she turned back and smiled at me. "Exactly. That's no way to treat a guest."

In her other hand, she had a six-pack of beer. I read the label: Becks. Becks beers.

My throat constricted. "*You* are Beers," I said slowly.

Another cheeky grin greeted me. "Yeah, of course." She rolled her eyes. "The day I met Jacko, she latched onto Becks beers as a way to remember my name because, in fact, I was drinking an alcohol-free one before I had to go on a shoot."

Oh, my God! Oh, my God! Oh, my God! My mind reeled. This could not be true.

"Sorry, you have to go. This was a mistake." I was practically pushing her back towards the door now.

"What?" For the first time, I saw her dimpled smile fade and turn to shock. "But, Jacko invited me."

I nodded. "You'll have to ring her and make up an excuse. Tell her you had a shoot or a headache or something." I tried to push her out the door.

She shook her head and twirled out of my grasp.

I heard the floorboards creak as Jacko stepped out of the bathroom into the kitchen part of the living room. She was dressed in jeans and her favourite turquoise polo shirt that set off her lovely dark tan and always made my breath catch. God, she looked good.

"Hey, I thought I heard something." She said with a big smile, and came towards us. I watched dumbfounded as she bypassed me and went to embrace Becks. "Welcome. Spot on time, as always." She waved Becks into the house. "Come, make yourself at home. Can I get you something to drink? I got some of that French wine you like."

"Yes, that would be lovely," Becks said and gave me an "I told you so" look behind Jacko's back. If she had been six years old, I could imagine she would have stuck her tongue out at me instead.

"Do you know how difficult it is to find French wine on a Greek island?" Jacko continued, leading Becks into the kitchen.

I was left standing, gaping like a goldfish at the door. Last night might have been my own wet dream come true. But tonight promised to be a horrific nightmare.

What followed were six of the tensest hours of my life. It was far worse than any business pitch session or Dragon's Den encounter I had ever had. I made a point of keeping my distance from Becks. She, on the other hand, seemed to be intent on sticking to me like acrylic on dry skin. And in that way that overly familiar people have, she kept touching me as she talked, resting a casual hand on my arm or on my knee whenever she could. Each touch burned like sulphuric acid. I had begun to think she was deliberately feeding off my discomfort.

My heart thumped high in my chest like it was about to pop out of my throat. I was literally sweating with anxiety, while all the time watching Jacko like a hawk, praying she would not pick up on the tension between Becks' and me. Luckily, Jacko seemed oblivious—oblivious to me. Instead, she seemed 120 percent focussed on flirting with Becks all night. My annihilation would also be my salvation.

When it was time for dinner, to my great relief, Jacko sat at the top of the table, placing herself in the middle with Becks and I on either side. It meant that Jacko could only observe one of us at a time, and it allowed me to call Jacko's attention away from Becks when Becks was acting inappropriately.

Unfortunately, Becks insisted on playing footsie with me under the table and, short of kicking her shins, there was no way of stopping her.

At one point, Jacko got up to get the pepper grinder from the kitchen counter. I knew that from there, Jacko would have a clear eye line to our feet. Unfortunately, Becks took this as an opportunity to be bolder, placing her feet on the chair between my knees.

I couldn't take it any longer. I snapped. I sprang up. In doing so, I knocked over my wine glass. The sudden crash brought Jacko to the rescue.

"We are in Greece, after all," Jacko teased while sweeping up the shattered glass. "It's tradition to break a few plates." I didn't miss the "what the hell is up with you" look she gave me, though.

I seized the opportunity. "Oh, no. Look. I spilled wine all over myself, too. Please excuse me." I escaped into the bathroom.

Behind the closed door, I sat down on the bath's edge, propping both palms on my knees to support my emotionally exhausted body. I tried to focus on my breathing. I was shaking like a leaf. I desperately needed to calm down, to keep it together, or Jacko would definitely figure it out. The look she had just given me while cleaning up the mess was not the first one of the night. She knew me too well. I could only hope that her natural egotism would prevail and she would merely take my strange behaviour as a sign of jealousy or something. If Jacko were to find out that I had slept with the one person she liked…. I could not imagine how she would react. I could not bear to find out.

Becks was really pushing her luck with me. She was probably getting off on the thrill of the secrecy. Could she really be unaware of what trouble she was causing? Or perhaps she just didn't care.

I rested my forehead in my hands. I couldn't think about all this right at that moment. I just had to get through the evening and then resolve to see Becks on her own and stop this ridiculousness once and for all. Then I could go back to trying to figure out how to break the news to Jacko. If I was lucky, perhaps Jacko needed never to find out.

As for me and Jacko….

I rubbed my eyes. That was too much to think about.

I got up and rinsed my face in the small basin. After drying off, I stared at my reflection in the mirror. Could I feign sickness? Truthfully, I looked pale, like I had seen a ghost.

No, that would definitely draw a veil over the evening and Jacko would never forgive me for ruining this opportunity with Becks. I hung the towel back on its hook, took a deep breath, slapped my cheeks to give them a bit of colour, and headed back out into the ring.

When I came back into the lounge, the party had moved from the constrained setting of the dining table to the unfortunately more relaxed arrangement of the couch by the fire. The only seat left for me was a tiny space on the couch directly next to Becks.

I could not possibly sit there.

"Anyone for some coffee?" I asked.

This caught Jacko's attention. She knew I never drank coffee in the evening. She gave me another quizzical look.

"Seems like a nice thing to have after such a wonderful meal," I said with a shrug.

Jacko seemed to accept my explanation.

"Actually, I will just make a cafetière, and then everyone can help themselves." I busied myself in the kitchen while keeping one pricked-up ear trained on their conversation.

Happily, Jacko and Becks were discussing the politics of a new group of Brits who had recently moved into the village. Apparently, there was a hierarchy within the expat community or at least a distinction between the original expats and the newcomers. Any newcomers had to earn their pips. Deceit and infidelity were regarded as two severe misdemeanours.

That counted me out, then. I couldn't help feeling that my apparent inability to be straight with Jacko about what happened with Becks equated to deceit. I could not quite understand why it all seemed so difficult. Fortunately, I was not hoping to contend for a place amongst the expat community any time soon.

I brought over the cafetière and three cups on a tray. I used the need to pour as an excuse to drag over a dining chair to sit on. Out of the corner of my eye, I caught Becks frowning at me. Clearly, she disliked being out-manoeuvred. Thankfully, Jacko used this as an opportunity to swiftly take up the space next to Becks.

Becks finished her coffee and, presumably sensing that she would not have another chance to up the ante in her game with me, called it a night, using the impending storm as a reason to get home sooner rather than later.

I would have liked the opportunity to give Becks a piece of my mind in private outside, but as Jacko was hell-bent on playing the attentive host and seeing Becks out, I stayed put and merely waved her off politely.

While Jacko was out, I sat in a stupor, unable to move. I felt absolutely exhausted from the nervous tension of the evening. I could not even contemplate what Becks was saying to Jacko while they were out there. I was more worried about the fact that when Jacko returned, she sure as hell was going to question me about my strange behaviour. What was I going to say?

So, it threw me completely when Jacko came back into the house looking like a Cheshire cat. I wondered if there was a God after all.

"I gather the goodbye went well?" I said, putting on a teasing tone.

Jacko nodded, looking like she had just got the cream—an unintended innuendo I really did not want to entertain at that moment.

"I think so," she said. She sat and turned her attention to me. "So?"

My heart sped up again. "So what?" I could feel my palms sweating.

"So? What do you think? About Beers?"

"Oh." I said, taking a deep breath. This was my moment. I had to tell her now or it would be too late. It will just get far, far worse if I didn't come clean. "Firstly, I didn't realise that Beers was Becks."

This brought another, even bigger, smile to Jacko's face. "Yeah, I quite like that I've got a special name for her. She seems to like it."

That was so Jacko—always wanting to be that little bit different, that little bit more special.

"But, yes, sorry. That must have been a bit confusing," she said.

I nodded. "Yes, so I didn't realise that when you invited Beers, you meant Becks." I knew I was stalling now.

Now was the moment of truth. I absolutely had to do it.

Jacko nodded again, still unable to drop her grin. She looked so pleased. So happy. She looked so hopeful. It would be like telling a child Father Christmas was your Uncle Fred. I couldn't bring myself to do it. I could not even open my mouth. Not right now. Instead, I stood up and gathered the coffee cups and the tray and took them to the kitchen sink.

"So? What do you think of her?" Jacko sounded impatient.

I stopped and turned back to Jacko, feigning thoughtfulness. I didn't really have a choice. I could hardly say "I'd kissed her and let her fuck me close to senseless…a few times…and I thought she was a little conniving, selfish, cheating, deceitful, chance taker…" Now, could I?

Instead, I nodded. "She's nice."

"And?" Jacko pressed, clearly wanting to know if I thought Becks liked her.

"And…I'm not sure who or what Becks likes."

I glanced at Jacko.

Then, a thought occurred to me. Maybe if we focussed on Jacko's relationship with Becks, maybe if I tried to help Jacko get the girl she wanted, maybe we could forget about what happened between us the previous evening.

The thought that I couldn't have Jacko in the way I wanted tore my heart apart, but maybe there would be a chance we could get through this and at least save our friendship. Would it be so bad to go back to being friends? Close friends. Like we were. I really was not prepared to lose my friend altogether.

"I mean, she seems to be quite a hard person to read," I said.

I was relieved to see Jacko nod. "Now you see why I wanted your opinion. I really have been trying to figure her out since the day I met her and I just can't. Sometimes I think she really likes me. Sometimes I think she just sees me as a handy person about the village."

In my years of business, the one key skill that I had developed was that of listener. People liked to talk about themselves and they liked you so much more for letting them do that. Sometimes that was all I needed to win me new business, as opposed to my competitors, who spent a lot of time and energy trying to make a good impression.

So, I allowed Jacko to talk, to vent, about all her frustration while trying to fathom Becks, and I agreed to keep a close eye on Becks and her interactions and, in due course, to give her further feedback.

What was I setting myself up for here?

As if the universe had sensed my devastation and my deep, dark, and desperate mood, I was not long in bed when a thunderstorm to end all thunderstorms broke out outside. Light from the electric storm filled the room with bright white flashes that intermittently obliterated all the shadows in my room. The rain pelted down so hard on the ceiling and windows, I feared they would shatter. The whole display made the incessant rain after our evening at Portokali seem like a drizzle. Or perhaps I had just been too preoccupied making love to Jacko to have noticed.

I knew I was not going to get much sleep.

I couldn't put on my light to read for fear that Jacko would realise I was awake and feel tempted to come to me for a heart-to-heart. I was afraid of talking to her right now.

I was afraid I would say something I would regret or I couldn't take back. It is what always happens in the movies. The guilty party gets interrogated by the police and resists until the end when they finally, inevitably, can't seem to help but spill the beans, choosing a clear conscience over their freedom. And this ultimately leads to their downfall. We, as the audience, all know that everything would have worked out fine if they'd just kept their mouths shut and said nothing. It was something I never understood. Now, I seemed doomed to follow suit.

1 2

*T*he storm continued well into the dawn.

When I couldn't lie there anymore, I got up and went to the kitchen to make myself a warm drink. Out the window at the front of the house, I saw huge torrents of water rushing down the path outside. Clearly the deluge of rain had caused the river to break its bank and it was in full flood.

A little while later, Jacko came downstairs, too. She was full of smiles with a spring in her step. She offered to make us a full cooked breakfast, which I was glad of, not so much because I needed the food, but because it kept Jacko busy, and I welcomed any distraction that would prevent us from having big conversations.

I busied myself with my iPad, checking my empty inbox again, and reading the latest news from around the world. I used to hate the news. It used to depress me—the madness that seemed to be our new world reality. Now, I found the mayhem and chaos out there strangely comforting. If nothing else, it made me feel better about my own life.

We had just finished breakfast, and I was helping Jacko dry the dishes when there came a knock at the front door.

Jacko slung the dish cloth over her shoulder and went to answer it while I continued to stack the plates and put things in the cupboards.

I almost dropped the glass in my hand when I heard Becks' voice. The nerve!

I turned to find her standing in the lounge. She looked like a drowned rat. Her jeans had been rolled up to her knees. She was barefoot in a raincoat with rolled-up sleeves over her top.

In a torrent of explanation, she told us that the river had broken its banks and flooded part of her house. Apparently, after she left us, she had spent most of the night trying to secure sandbags and bolsters to bank and divert the water away from the house. To no avail. The water had tripped all the electricity.

"Do either of you know anything about electricity, please? I really need to turn it back on."

I almost felt sorry for her. I shook my head. "I'm very sorry. I'm useless at DIY."

Jacko, on the other hand, prided herself on her DIY skills and came to the rescue. "I know a bit. Let me come and see what I can do."

I panicked. I couldn't allow Jacko and Becks to spend more time alone together. I couldn't risk Becks letting anything slip to Jacko about us before I had the chance to come clean.

"Let me just grab some clothes and then I'll come with you, too," I said. "Maybe I can at least help move sandbags."

Becks looked very happy at the suggestion. I didn't look at Jacko.

I rushed up the stairs and changed quickly out of my pyjamas and into a pair of jeans, T-shirt, and anorak.

During our time together, Becks had never taken me back to her place. She seemed to prefer to limit our encounters to clandestine outdoor locations. I could now guess why.

Her house was a small three-roomed building comprising a living room, bathroom, and bedroom. It was situated in a field in the middle of the Kampos only a few metres away from what in summer would have been a dry riverbed. Now, however, on account of the storm, the field had transformed into a marsh, and the level of water, judging by the watermark on the outside of the house, had reached mid-thigh height. Luckily, once the storm had stopped, it had receded rapidly to a foot high.

Inside the house, the devastation was shocking. The water was lapping at the walls, and the furniture had been wrecked. Lighter items, like pillows and books, bobbed and floated around in the murky brown water. In the corner of the living-room, a small telly stood half-submerged in water. Similarly, in the bedroom, which was a step lower down from the living area, everything was still covered by water, with only half the pine bed's headboard visible. Even if the river subsided rapidly over the next few hours, it would take days, if not weeks, for the house and furniture to dry out properly.

"What a shit storm!" Jacko said with feeling.

Even I felt sorry for Becks. But if this was what life in the Kampos was like every time there was a bit of rain, I could not understand why people would live here. For the same reason, I could also not understand why people lived near the coast, which was frequently wrecked by tsunamis and seasonal tidal changes that annihilated everything in its path. Could it be a sign of a certain type of person who wanted the impossible? I mentally slapped myself for being so cynical at such a time.

Jacko glanced around, looking for something in the living room. Then she spotted it. I saw her go to open the fuse box. I was about to question the logic of touching electricity standing knee high in water, but refrained. Jacko would not have appreciated the mothering.

"All the fuses have tripped," she said. "It's best that way. You don't want to reset them until everything has dried out."

Becks looked despondent, but nodded.

I really did feel sorry for her.

"There's not much else to do around here except wait," Jacko said, and surveyed the room with her hands on her hips. "I think you will have to find somewhere else to stay for a few days."

Becks nodded again. Jacko put an arm around Becks and kissed the top of her head.

"I tell you what," she said, "why don't you grab a change of clothes and come stay with us for a few days? I'm sure Spice won't mind." Jacko looked at me.

Although I could hardly breathe, I tried to smile and nodded. "Of course, not." I forced the words out.

"Spice is in the spare room but the couch in the living room is a sleeper couch. As long as you don't mind sleeping in the living room, you'd be very welcome." Jacko came across like the concerned friend, but I could imagine that secretly her pulse was racing at the prospect of having Beers under her roof. Or was I being unfair?

After only a moment's hesitation, I saw Becks' face light up. All I could think was, would I actually survive the next few days?

Half an hour later, we were all three sat around Jacko's dining table, enjoying a hot bowl of Jacko's famous fish stew.

Clearly, I was not the only one who hadn't slept a wink last night. By 8.00 p.m., after a last glass of wine, Becks yawned loudly. Both Jacko and I took the hint. I, for one, was very relieved. The prospect of spending another tense evening with Jacko and Becks gave me collywobbles.

I was in my room getting ready for bed when there came a soft knock at my door. To my horror, it was Becks.

"What are you doing here?" I whispered, very aware that the wall between the two rooms was temporary and, unlike the outer, almost half a metre thick, stone perimeter, it was paper thin.

"I just came to say good night," Becks stepped up close to me and kissed me on the lips.

I stood stunned.

"And I just wanted to say thank you for letting me stay. Not only is it very kind, but I'm also pleased it gives me a bit of time with you. I couldn't have imagined a better outcome to such a disaster."

I didn't know how to respond. I wanted to say it wasn't my idea and, in fact, if it had been up to me, she would be very far away from this house right now. But I couldn't bring myself to do that. Instead, like the coward I was, I just nodded.

"Please, you can't be here." I gently pushed her back towards the door.

She looked perplexed. "Jacko is an adult. If we're together, she shouldn't have a problem with it."

I could feel myself scream in my head. How could she not get what was going on? I really was not going to be the one to break it to Becks about Jacko's crush on her, or my crush on Jacko, or any of the madness of the situation. More to the point, I couldn't let Jacko find her in my room!

"I can't. Not now. We can talk in the morning," I said quickly and pushed her more urgently back out into the hall outside the bedrooms.

It looked like she might leave. I held my breath. Then, she paused for a few seconds and I dreaded she might change her mind. Thankfully, she turned and headed back to the living room.

To my horror, as she passed Jacko's door, she stepped on one of the creaking floorboards. My heart nearly stopped.

My eyes darted towards Jacko's closed bedroom door. All I needed now was for Jacko to come out and find us both in the hallway, looking guilty.

I motioned for Becks to keep going. She did.

But I had to think quickly. I had no doubt that Jacko must have heard the creak. I took a few quick steps towards her door and knocked quietly, then I opened it. It was dark inside. I stepped into the room.

Inside Jacko's room, the streetlight partly illuminated the room like it did in mine. I heard, rather than saw, Jacko stir.

She sat up. "What's going on?"

I realised I had woken her and regretted my guilt-ridden assumption instantly.

"Jacko, it's just me." The thought that Jacko could have hoped it was Becks thumped me like a blow to the gut. "It's Spice," I added quickly.

"What is it? What's the matter?" Jacko asked with urgency in her voice.

I sat down on the bed next to her. "Sorry, I didn't realise you were already asleep." I said. "Jacko…"

Now that I was there, I didn't know what to say. My head was racing. Was this the moment I came clean? Or what other excuse would I have to be sitting on the edge of her bed in the middle of the night?

I cupped her hand where it rested on the bed next to me. For some reason, I needed to connect with her, to feel her warmth.

Jacko turned towards me, tucking her feet in underneath her in a cross-legged position. Then, she held my hand in both of hers.

"Look, Spice, I'm really sorry about what happened between us." Her voice sounded serious in the dark, and that was the last thing I expected her to say. "I mean, I'm sorry it happened. It should never have. I mean, it was nice and everything, but we can't have it happen again. Not now. Not with Becks downstairs."

The horror swept over me like a wave. Is that why Jacko thought I was there? She thought I was there to get into her bed. I shook my head profusely in the dark. The bed wobbled from my motion. "No, no. That's not why I'm here."

Even just from her silhouette, I could see Jacko's demeanour change from cautious tension to relief. "Good. Good."

I could feel her gaze seeking me out in the dark. She let go of my hand. "So, what's up?"

How was I supposed to answer that?

"I just came… I wanted to say…that it was very kind of you to… about what you did today… It was very nice and kind. It was very good of you to invite Becks to stay." As the words left my mouth, they felt so hollow and lame.

I could see Jacko wait for me to finish. I knew she was waiting for more—something significant. "I'm sorry, that's all I want to say. I didn't realise I'd be waking you up."

"Not a problem. I'm sorry we have an extra guest during your visit. But it couldn't really be helped."

I nodded in the dark. "I'll leave you to get some sleep." I got up and fled from her bedroom as quickly as I could.

1 3

*J*acko was an early riser. I had heard her alarm through the thin walls a few mornings previously.

At 6:55 a.m., I was pacing outside her door, listening for the telltale beeps of her mobile phone. Bang on seven, I felt the vibrations. She must have put her phone on silent, hoping not to wake the entire household.

I stepped forward and gently knocked on her door. Before she answered, I opened the door and went in.

Jacko was still lying in bed, rubbing her eyes. At hearing the door open, she looked up, blurry eyed, trying to focus.

"Goodness, my bedroom has become busier than Central Station." She laughed at her own joke. "I should be so lucky."

I smiled, trying to seem lighthearted, but what I had to say weighed too heavily on me to pull it off. I sat down on the bed as I had done the previous night.

Jacko must have realised something was the matter. She sat up and looked at me expectantly. "What's up?" Her concern was very touching, and I almost hugged her for it.

"Jacko, I've been thinking." I tried to keep my voice as steady as I could. "I think I should move into the Sappho Hotel for the rest of my stay."

If I'd been in a more jovial mood, I would have laughed at Jacko's shocked expression. I gathered it was the last thing she had expected me to say, and it took her a few seconds to process my words. Then, she immediately started shaking her head.

I held up my hand to stop her from speaking. I really needed her to hear me.

"Look, Jacko, we know you're interested in Becks. I think it would be better if I gave you two some space—if I was out of the way. This, the fact that she's here, is an opportunity for you to spend some real time together and see if this, I mean you two, could go somewhere."

Jacko continued to shake her head profusely. "Absolutely not!" She got up and threw on her robe.

I had forgotten she slept in the nude. Right now, the sight of her body almost made me blush. It was not like I was unaccustomed to seeing her like that. She had always been very comfortable naked in my presence, since very early in our friendship, and it never bothered me before. But somehow, after the other night, my innocence had been stripped away.

I closed my eyes. "Jacko, please. Just listen to me."

"Absolutely not," she repeated, more slowly and more definitively. "I will not have you leave. You are my guest. This is the first time in I don't know how many years that you've come to visit me. I'm not making you homeless by sending you to a hotel, for *any* reason, and certainly not so I can explore 'an opportunity' with someone else. If anything more is possible with Becks, then there will be plenty of time for that later. Not while you're here visiting me."

I was touched by her ardour. Unfortunately, it didn't help my predicament. I honestly considered coming clean completely and really telling her how I feel. How much it would hurt to see her and Becks get together right before my eyes, never mind the turmoil my history with Becks was causing, and thus how forcing me to stay was so much worse than allowing me to go. Worse for everyone.

"This house is big enough for all three of us. It will only be for a few more days while Beck's house dries out," Jacko said.

Even if it was one more day, it would be the toughest day of my entire life if I allowed Jacko to talk me into staying. "Jacko, really—"

"Absolutely not, Spice. I will not hear of it." Jacko got up and walked out of the room and I, like a child needing to plead with a parent, got up and followed her, still hoping, praying that I could change her mind.

We got downstairs to find Becks in the process of getting up.

"Morning," she said, and trotted past us to the bathroom. "Sorry, can't talk. Water on the brain." She shut the bathroom door behind her with a bang.

"Jacko, please listen." I whispered, not wanting Becks to overhear our conversation, but feeling quite desperate.

"Spice, I've given you my answer. I will not have it."

The bathroom door swung open and Becks stepped out. She stopped and glanced from me to Jacko and back at me.

"This reminds me of the moment I walked in on my sister, at age eighteen, telling my not-very-sympathetic parents that she was pregnant. What have I missed?"

Jacko held my gaze, warning me. She shook her head. "Absolutely not," she said, and continued to fill the kettle.

Becks took a few more steps into the kitchen. She looked directly at me and then back at Jacko. "Absolutely not what?"

I shook my head. I really didn't want to share this conversation with Becks. I turned and sat down at the dining table.

Clearly, Jacko didn't have the same need for discretion. "Spice just suggested that she move out to a hotel, to give us more 'space.'"

"Space for what?" Becks asked, clearly not understanding and sounding a little panicked.

"But I said I'll have none of it. This house is big enough for the three of us to spend a few days together. Besides, it could be fun," Jacko smiled. "I can get some marshmallows and we can toast them at midnight and pretend we're back in boarding school." Jacko laughed and turned to get the coffee mugs.

Becks turned and threw me a sharp look.

"Right, that's settled, then," Jacko said. "I'm going to go get dressed while the coffee brews and I'll be back to make us a veggie fry-up for breakfast. I don't know about you two, but I'm starving." Jacko bounded back up the stairs to her room, taking two steps at a time.

Becks waited somewhat impatiently for Jacko to disappear out of earshot before she marched up to me. "What the hell! What is all this about?"

I shook my head. I really had hoped Jacko would keep her mouth shut, but clearly nothing between Jacko and me was sacred anymore.

"What's going on? If I was suspicious in nature, I'd be wondering if you're deliberately trying to avoid me," Becks hissed.

I shook my head.

"If so... you're singing from a very different song sheet compared to when we were at the lake and the beach. What's happened? Why do I feel like I'm now getting the brush-off?"

I shook my head again. "Becks, I'm sorry. It should never have happened." I suddenly felt like I was channeling Jacko.

Becks' face contorted. "What do you mean it 'should' never have happened? It did. You make it sound like it was a passing accident, like bumping into the curb or knocking over a glass of wine. We shared more than a one-night stand. Or is that all I was to you? Do you always just use people like that?"

"Becks."

"Don't Becks me. Is that what this is all about?"

I shook my head. A splitting headache had begun just behind my eyes. "I mean it was... but now that Jacko's back..." I didn't know how to finish the sentence.

"With Jacko back, what?"

I could see Becks' brow crease under her blonde fringe that was still a bit tousled from sleep. Then, her face changed. "Ooooh." The single world stretched out, filling the surrounding room.

I was not sure what she had concluded, but it instantly worried me. "Becks, it's not what you think."

Beck scoffed. "I think it's exactly what I think."

Right then, Jacko came bounding down the stairs. "So, who's hungry?"

"Is the Pope Catholic?" Becks said brightly, like she had not a care in the world.

Jacko glanced at me, looking for agreement, and I nodded.

"I'll just get dressed and then I can help break some eggs," I said.

"No, no. Not necessary." Jacko said, waving me off. "I won't have my guests slave in my kitchen. But go get dressed, both of you. That gives me a bit of time to work my magic."

I trundled up the stairs, relieved to have a few minutes to myself to recover and think what to do now. If anything, I would have to prepare myself for probably one of the most challenging days of my life.

When I came back downstairs, I found Becks still in the shorts and tank top she had slept in, leaning forward against the kitchen central island table opposite where Jacko was chopping onions. She had her hands pressed down on either side of her on the counter, which had the effect of pressing her bosoms together, making them look larger and accentuating her cleavage. She was laughing at something Jacko had said. If I had been in a better mood, the scene would almost have seemed comical. The two of them flirting and giggling. Or, rather, Jacko was just being her natural charming self, while Becks, on the other hand, had somehow morphed into a 1960s debutant, fake laughing at the most eligible bachelor's every joke.

I watched for a few moments, almost mesmerised by the charade. Surely Jacko could see through this.

What felt worse was that I was suddenly the intruder.

Can this day get any worse? Not only do I have to endure being in their company, but now I have to watch Becks and Jacko flirt.

Breakfast was as excruciating as I had expected.

In one respect, it was a relief that Becks' focus had shifted from me. In another, it was like watching a train wreck taking place in slow motion. By then, I had no doubt what Becks was up to. She had clearly deduced that there was something more between Jacko and me, or that I wanted there to be. It seemed she had decided to sabotage anything between Jacko and me by putting on a very elaborate charade to make me jealous.

Either way, she was childish, petty, and revengeful.

I would have liked to warn Jacko, not only about what type of person Becks clearly was, but also to guard her heart. I couldn't bear the idea of seeing Jacko get hurt, but my hands were tied. I couldn't bear to hurt Jacko either.

14

During breakfast, Jacko had offered to go to have a look at Becks' house with her again to see how the drying-out process was progressing. They both turned and looked at me expectantly.

I feigned a grimace. "Oh, I'm so sorry. I forgot to say that I need to call my lawyer about the sale of my business. It seems there's a glitch."

I saw Jacko frown. "Oh, what? When? I thought that was all done and dusted?"

I shook my head and shrugged. "Yes, I thought so, too, but I got a text message late last night. Arnold needs to speak to me this morning. Anyway, it's all very inane stuff I won't bore you with."

"Wow, Arnold texted you after we went to bed?" Jacko persisted.

I shrugged again. "That's one of the reasons I chose these guys to handle the sale. They seem to work twenty-four/seven. Very good service."

I thought for a moment Jacko was not going to drop it, but finally she nodded and shrugged in Becks' direction. "Seems it'll just be the two of us."

Becks smiled. "I think that should be more than enough."

I almost wanted to vomit.

Once they had left, and I had the house to myself, I felt like I wanted to throw a party from sheer relief. Finally, I could breathe. However, my elation did not last long. I desperately needed to find a way out of there. I paced the width of the living room, running my fingers through my hair.

"Come on, Terry, you've got yourself out of tighter situations before," I said to myself. I had to admit, this was a pretty tight situation. Maybe my impromptu excuse of Arnold's call could be more useful than I thought.

I picked up my phone and pressed the number-three autodial. I only had three numbers on autodial. The first was Jacko, but I hardly used that since we video called most of the time. The second was Arnold. The third was for Nora, my neighbour, who kept an eye on my flat whenever I was away. She was also probably the closest person I had to a friend in London. Calling it a friendship was a bit like calling a Morris Minor a nephew to a Rolls Royce. Our friendship extended as far as brief hellos in the stairwell, and occasionally she had invited herself over for a drink or a cup of tea when she knew I was home. On the odd occasion, she had even brought me dinner. Clearly, I appealed to her mothering instinct.

"Hi, Nora, it's me."

"Me who?" Her gravelly voice crackled over the phone.

"Terry, Terry Cox. Your neighbour."

I heard her shriek on the other side of the phone. Clearly, getting a call from me was a thrilling novelty.

I was very aware that Jacko and Becks could return any minute, so I had to stay focussed. "Nora, sorry I can't speak for very long. I just need to ask you a huge favour." My serious tone obviously helped focus her attention.

"Anything, darling. You know me."

"I need you to ring me back later, at around…" I did the calculations in my head, "about 4:30 p.m. your time."

There was a moment's silence. "Okay," she said hesitantly. "Any specific reason?"

"I need you to pretend to be Arnold, if that's okay. I haven't got time to explain everything now," I said. "I need you to just trust me and go with the flow, if you can."

"Sure, honey. In my day, I was an actor. So, yes, I can do an impromptu telephone conversation. Four thirty, you say?"

"Yes, please, Nora. I owe you one."

I had just put the phone down in time before Jacko and Becks walked in through the door, all smiles and affected giggles.

"You two seem very happy." I couldn't help myself. "I guess the drying-out is progressing well?"

Jacko chuckled. "Actually, no. It turns out that we had forgotten to remove the sandbags from in front of the outside door, trapping the water inside the house." Jacko laughed and nudged Becks.

"Silly me," Beck said and shrugged.

I could smack Becks.

And, I couldn't help wonder if she was really as innocent in that mistake as she pretended.

I willed the next few hours to pass by as quickly as possible until Nora's call. Why had I asked her to ring so late? Could I feign a headache until then?

———

The hours dragged by. I tried really hard not to keep glancing at the time on my phone. Unfortunately, Jacko knew me too well.

"You waiting for something?" she asked.

"Yes, sorry," I said. "As I mentioned, I spoke to my lawyer this morning, and they said they would get back to me later today. So, sorry if I seem a little distracted. It's quite an urgent matter." The moment I said that, I thought I had probably gone too far.

"What's going on?" Jacko sounded concerned, triggering more guilt.

"Oh, no, nothing. It's too complicated to go into right now. Besides, I don't want to ruin such a lovely day by talking about work. I've been doing that for too long." And although that certainly was true, I could see the blatant irony of resorting to work as an excuse to get myself out of a social situation. I drained the last of my non-alcoholic beer. I didn't trust myself on alcohol at that moment. I wanted to have a clear head for when Nora rang.

At 6.32 p.m., my phone rang.

I jumped and snatched it, startling everybody.

"Excuse me," I said, "I really have to take this." I looked at Jacko apologetically. At that point, I was glad I had primed them earlier about the call, because now Jacko just blinked at me in an understanding manner. I took the phone and moved off a little, giving the appearance of needing privacy. However, I made sure not to walk too far away. After all, the whole point of the call was to get Jacko to overhear.

"Hello, this is your scheduled telephone service," Nora said on the other end.

"Oh, hello, Arnold. Yes, yes. I can hear you. Can you hear me?" I pretended to press my finger into my other ear and listen more closely. "Yes, now I can hear you clearly. Yes, thank you for ringing back."

Nora's voice crackled again. "I have no idea what you want me to say, but I'm just going to fill in the pauses."

"So, tell me, Arnold. What happened?"

"Well, since the last time we spoke," Nora continued, "young Billy, do you remember him? The strapping young lad with the dark tan who works as lifeguard in Ibiza or somewhere exotic, came over for the afternoon to surprise me. Isn't that sweet? Anyway, we ended up having rampant sex—"

"Thank you, Arnold. Thanks for telling me in so much detail." I couldn't believe Nora was sharing this with me.

"Well, unless you want to tell me what this is all about, in which case, considering my extensive acting experience, I could improvise more appropriately—"

"Yes, thanks. I shall do that next time."

"So, unless you want me to carry on for the next fifteen to twenty minutes telling you about my delicious extracurricular activities of the afternoon, I suggest you get the point."

"Oh, I see. Gosh, well, in that case, it's urgent. We need to get this resolved as quickly as possible or it could end up being quite an unpleasant experience."

"Well, only an unpleasant experience if you're not into that kind of thing, which I'm guessing you're not."

I had never discussed my sexuality with Nora.

"Although," Nora continued, "I have not seen much evidence of you getting much action on front—"

"Yes, thank you, Arnold." I had to really stop myself from calling Nora by her name and telling her to behave. "I see. Thank you very much for sharing your views. Yes, there doesn't seem to be much choice. I'll try to get there as soon as possible."

"Get where?"

"I'll sort out the details and let you know when I arrive." I made a point of saying the last few words loudly enough to be heard clearly. I could sense Jacko's ears prick up and their otherwise bubbly, more-than-slightly inebriated, conversation die down.

Bingo! Desired effect achieved.

"Thanks again, Arnold. I really appreciate this. You are a lifesaver."

"You bloody better be appreciating this. I don't interrupt good sex for anyone."

"Absolutely. Put it on the tab. Thank you. I'll see you soon."

I cut the call before Nora could say anything else.

I took a deep breath and turned towards Jacko and Becks, where they were now openly staring and waiting for me to speak.

"What's going on?" Jacko asked, clearly worried about me.

I took a deep breath and tried to imagine what it really would feel like if what I was about to say was true. I would be devastated.

"It seems there's an issue with the final paperwork for the sale of the business."

Jacko's face fell. "Oh, no!" She got up and came over to me and rested a concerned hand on my arm. "Are you okay?"

I nodded. "It seems I planned my holiday a little prematurely. I'm going to have to cut it short and head back home to try and sort this out."

"I am so sorry," Jacko said, giving my arm a little squeeze.

My insides twisted with guilt at deceiving my friend like that. I momentarily wavered and considered the alternative. I shuddered at the thought of the devastation that would cause and decided that this little white lie about having to go back to London was not the worst price to pay. I knew at some point in the future, I would need to explain the truth, but not right then and not in the presence of Becks.

"So, when do you have to go?" Jacko asked.

"Unfortunately, as soon as I can."

"The next direct flight to London is not before the weekend," Jacko said.

I shook my head. The prospect of staying in this awkwardness for any longer than absolutely necessary was unbearable. "I need to get back as soon as possible."

"Flights to Athens run every day," Becks said, probably trying to be helpful.

Jacko turned towards me and took my hands in hers. Her expression was serious. "Please don't rush off tomorrow morning. I finally have you here after years. Please, stay for a few more days."

My heart almost broke at Jacko's earnestness. I really did love her with all my heart and I was so touched that me being there meant so much to her, too. I squeezed her hands gently. "Jacko, I'm sorry." I wished that I could convey how truly sorry I was for everything.

"Please," she said, "just stay one more night. We can go to the Greek evening for one last time. See it as your farewell party."

I would say this about Jacko—she was persistent and very persuasive, and I could not disappoint her even more. I nodded.

15

*F*rom the moment I mentioned that I needed to leave, I noticed Jacko's focus change and was from then on directed on me almost exclusively. I can't say I disliked the feeling. However, I was also acutely aware of the ominous, jealous vibes radiating off Becks. Every time I looked at Becks, her face seemed more clouded, her breathing seemed more huffy, her attempts at conversation with Jacko more desperate. She was clearly not coping with not being the centre of mine or Jacko's attention. This was a side of Becks I hadn't expected and it made me very uncomfortable, to the extent that I almost regretted my decision not to leave immediately. I had to keep reminding myself that I was doing this for Jacko.

At the Greek night, Jacko walked in with me, leaving Becks to follow in our wake. Anyone looking would have assumed Jacko and I were together and Becks was a hanger-on.

Unfortunately, Jacko excused herself and headed to the bar, leaving Becks and me on our own. Becks saw her opportunity. She sidled up next to me.

"So, I guess this is it for us, then?" she said, sounding friendlier than she had since I discovered she was Jacko's Beers.

I nodded. "I'm afraid so."

She looked sad, and my heart twinged. I had to admit that none of this was really Becks' fault. It was not fair that she was the object of my anger and disdain.

"Becks, it was really lovely to get to know you and I had a wonderful time with you." All of that was true. It was not her fault that things between Jacko and me had got complicated. The truth was, Jacko and I were complicated from the start. I just had not realised it.

Jacko reappeared, carrying two glasses of wine. "Sorry, Beers, they seem to have run out of Becks, so I didn't know what else to get you. I think you might have to go see what they have for yourself," Jacko said, handing me a wineglass.

I could almost see something shift in Becks' expression and I felt even more sorry for her. It was horrid to feel like a third wheel in any situation.

I was about to offer to go to get Becks her drink of choice when our lovely host, Sophia, came past. She wanted Jacko to help her with something related to the sound system. For some reason, everybody thought that Jacko knew everything about music. The more Jacko tried to explain that her speciality was select stringed instruments and nothing electronic, the more they seemed to think she was the sound guru to call on.

"So that's all it was to you? A holiday fling?" Becks said the moment we were alone again. The malice in her tone caught me completely off guard. "After what I thought were wonderful days that we spent together, me showing you lovely places, taking time out for picnics and not to mention making glorious love to you anywhere and everywhere…. This is it? You going to leave and return to your life in London like nothing happened?" Becks picked up Jacko's glass where she had left it standing on the table near me.

I could feel this situation was starting to spiral out of control. "Becks, look—"

"I'm not just some kind of tool people can use to scratch an itch and then throw away like it meant nothing." She took a large swig of Jacko's wine.

"Becks, that's not true. I did not—"

"Yes, it is. And don't think I can't see what's really going on here. I see how you look at her. Was I just a way to make her jealous?"

I scoffed. "Nothing of the sort!" I realise that my voice had hitched, and that we were on the verge of attracting unwanted attention.

"I will not be part of your games," Becks said. The irony struck me like an iron fist.

"Games? What games?" Jacko's voice surprised us both.

"I was just saying I wonder whether there will be any Greek games tonight?" I stared at Becks in a silent warning. I prayed that she was not stupid enough to allow this to get completely out of hand.

Once again, I was reminded that there was no God, or at least She had more important things to do than listen to my prayers.

"No, actually," Becks said.

My blood ran cold. *Please* don't do this, Becks!

"I was just telling Spice that I'm no longer going to play her little games."

And there it was.

Jacko's brow furrowed.

I closed my eyes and awaited the inevitable.

"Spice here has been playing me to make you jealous. Or, perhaps, to stop whatever might be happening between you and me. She obviously knows that you and I like each other. So, she came on to me at the Greek night while you were away."

"That is nonsense," I exclaimed.

I saw Jacko's eyes darken as she stared at each of us. "What?"

"Go on, tell her," Becks taunted me.

I shook my head. This was my worst nightmare come true.

"Tell me what?" Jacko asked me. "Is this true, Spice?"

"Yes, it is true," Becks interjected. "Would I lie? Tell her how that first night we ended up at the lake. Or should I? And then what happened again the next day on the beach—"

"Spice? Is this true?" Jacko's eyes bored into me.

I pinched the bridge of my nose. How was I going to explain any of this? No matter what I said, Becks was right. I had lied to Jacko. I had been deceitful. No matter which way one looked at this, I was guilty. And the more I protested, the more guilty I would seem to Jacko.

Obviously, my silence spoke for itself.

"I don't believe this," Jacko said, her dark eyes almost sparking with rage. If they could shoot daggers, they would have. "Please tell me this is not true."

I could not find the words to explain that it was Becks who had come on to me.

In my peripheral vision, I saw Becks lean back against the table and cross her arms. Clearly, her work there was done. She could lean back and let this play out. She was practically smirking as she watched my world crumble. God help me, if I had anything to do with it, she was going to have a very short life.

Jacko turned away from us and rubbed her brow, as if deciding what to do. Hands on hips, she turned back to me. I thought she was going to say something, but clearly she thought better of it. She shook her head and stormed towards the door.

I thumped my glass down on the table and ran after her.

"Jacko," I called, as she headed down the road. She didn't even falter.

"Jacko, please, listen to me. I can explain."

Finally, Jacko turned towards me. The fury and hurt in her expression was almost frightening.

"You can explain?" she hissed. "Okay, I have one simple question for you. You knew I liked Beers, and you slept with her?"

"It wasn't like that."

"One simple question. Did you sleep with her?" Jacko stood with her hands on her hips glaring at me.

I could not hold her gaze. I didn't know how to even begin to explain.

She shook her head, casting her eyes towards the heavens.

"How could you?"

She turned, got into her car, and drove off, leaving me standing, stunned, watching her taillights disappear into the distance.

By the time I had walked back to Jacko's house, I found her sitting on the couch with a large bottle of Jack Daniels, only a quarter full. I recognised it as one of the bottles she had bought at duty-free on her return from Moscow.

"Jacko, I—"

Jacko held up a hand and didn't even look at me. "I don't want to talk."

I sighed and went up to my room.

My flight was not until the morning but, I could not bear spending a night like this with Jacko. Especially not my last night. I packed my suitcase.

Twenty minutes later, I came down the stairs, suitcase in hand. The taxi to Mytilene, which would take me to my hotel, was already waiting outside.

What do I say? This seems to be the recurring question I had asked myself since I had arrived in Greece.

Jacko was sitting there on the couch, a closed book—deaf to me. I sighed and headed to the door. I could not leave and not say anything. This might be the last opportunity I had to talk to my best friend.

I turned back.

"I know you don't want to talk to me right now. I understand that. But before I leave through this door, I need you to know that I am truly sorry, Jacko." I stared at her, looking for even the smallest movement.

"Jacko, I really didn't know Becks was your Beers. You have to believe me. I would never…" The words died on my lips. I could not even express what had happened. "The truth is, I never wanted Becks. Not really. I came here to spend time with you, then you had to go. At first, I thought it was a good idea to let my hair down and try to have some fun for the first time in years. Then, you came back and slowly things became clear to me, not least during the night that we spent together. I realised that what I really want is not just 'some fun'. I wanted you."

I waited, hoping Jacko would at least acknowledge what I had said. She didn't even blink.

"It's always been you I wanted, Jacko. I had just not realised it." I swallowed back the tears.

"Anyway, the point is, I just wanted you to know that I am sorry for sleeping with Becks and I really didn't know she was your Beers. If I had, none of this would have happened. I would never want to hurt you. I hope you believe me."

Jacko still seemed no more responsive than a fibreglass mannequin.

There was nothing more I could do or say. I turned and left.

16

Almost twenty hours after I left Jacko, I landed at Heathrow. From there I caught a taxi home. Under normal circumstances, I would have taken the Tube, but I was too tired and desperately looking forward to a night in my own bed.

Well, that was my intention, anyway.

Unfortunately, the fates had different ideas.

Barely fifteen minutes after I got home, there came a knock on my door.

Nora, my neighbour, a fifty-five-year-old terminally straight, wealthy widow, stood in my doorway holding a martini. She was dressed in a negligee and matching silk gown. Her make-up and hair looked immaculate, as if she had stepped out of a black-tie affair. I could only assume she had gone to all that effort for the booty call of another in her string of young male suitors.

"Look, Nora, I'm exhausted. Can this wait?"

She held up a slim, manicured index finger. "This will not take long, but I have hardly slept a wink since that phone call you asked me to make for you. You owe me this much. I need to at least know what kind of trouble you're in."

Before I could protest, she pushed past me and made her way to my couch.

I sighed and closed the door behind her. I had learnt from previous experience that the best way to get rid of Nora was to indulge her and get whatever it was she was asking for over with as quickly as possible.

In the kitchen, I poured myself a large glass of white wine. "Would you like one?" I asked.

In response, she held up her martini.

I went over and plonked down on the armchair next to the couch Nora was lounging on. She watched me intently.

"Okay, spill. Give up go the goods. What's going on?"

I took a large sip of my wine and sighed deeply. Where to start? "I realised I was in love with my best friend, I slept with her, and I betrayed her, not necessarily in that order."

"Oh, my goodness, and all that within a few weeks? No wonder you needed to be airlifted out."

I couldn't hold it back anymore and I burst into tears. Until that moment, it was as if I had been living in a dream, holding the waters at bay. But now, in the safety of my armchair, unfortunately in front of Nora, the severity of the situation finally hit home.

Nora sprang up and came to sit on the armrest next to me and rubbed my shoulder. "There, girl. Let it all out. Is this Jacko we're talking about?" She said Jacko's name like it was a bad taste in her mouth.

I nodded.

"I always thought she was bad news." She rubbed my shoulder. "Did you tell her you're in love with her?"

I couldn't bring myself to speak. I merely nodded.

"She didn't want you?"

I nodded again.

"Well, then, it serves her right that you found somebody better." It was clear that Nora had not understood the problem.

"If only it were that simple." I rested my face in my free hand.

"Well, as you English would say," she said in her best American drawl, "I think this one calls for a cup of tea." She got up and went to the bathroom, reappearing a few minutes later with a large box of tissues that I kept next to the basin. She handed them over before she made us both a cuppa, allowing me a few minutes to dry my eyes and compose myself.

Although I didn't drink the tea and continued to sip my wine, I proceeded to tell Nora the whole story.

Finally, once I had finished, she tutted softly, got up, and gave me another very warm hug. I guess there was not much she could have said about the situation.

"My dear girl, you have to remember, there will always be other fish in the sea," she said.

I shook my head. "Not like Jacko. She's my best friend... has been my anchor since I was twenty-one. I cannot live without her in my life."

"I know that's how it feels now. And if you choose to, know that in time you will make new friends. I can't guarantee you will necessarily fall in love again. I have made a point not to. But life, as they say, carries on for those still breathing."

The poignancy of Nora's words struck me. After all, she knew what she was talking about, having lost her beloved Oscar to cancer fifteen years previously.

On impulse, I leant over and gave Nora a hug.

"Thank you," I said softly.

She pulled away and nodded, a fleeting, sad look in her eyes. Then, she seemed to shake herself off.

"Onwards and upwards. You know where I am if you need a cocktail or a cuppa." She got up and let herself out of my flat.

***

My grandmother warned me once never to tempt fate. I should have listened to her.

The day after I arrived home, I received a phone call from the real Arnold. Turned out there really were complications in the paperwork, but unlike in my fake scenario, he didn't feel the need to ring me in Greece. I had, after all, paid him enough in service fees to finance the purchase of his new house in Highgate, so he had taken it upon himself to sort out the legalities and the paperwork before he rang to tell me.

The only thing left was for him to bring the new documents round for me to sign. It was not urgent. The buyers were aware, and all had been dealt with. He said he would pop round to my flat around lunchtime on Saturday. I set a reminder in my calendar to get out of my pyjamas on Saturday morning, and went back to bed.

The next couple of days consisted of Netflix, pizza, and heart-wrenching tunes. Once a day Nora would pop in to bring me something green to eat, which I stuffed in the fridge and ignored.

At fifty-five, she had a thirty-two-year-old figure, which she put down to her vegetarian diet. When I asked her about how her alcohol consumption fits into this healthy regime, she pointed out that wines were made from grapes and vodka and gin from grain.

I could hardly argue.

"Sounds like a fairly balanced diet," I said, and poured myself yet another glass of wine to take back to bed with me.

17

*S*aturday morning arrived and I hauled my bones out of bed at 11.00 a.m., had a shower and finally got dressed. Arnold was due just before lunch.

Too lazy to actually prepare lunch myself, I called in to the local restaurant for a gourmet delivery. I had used their services before on a number of occasions, on account of not being a great fan of spending time in the kitchen.

At 12.30, lunch arrived, followed by Arnold at 12.45. He was a short, thin, very well-sculpted gay man of a certain age with deep furrows in his brow.

"God, you look like shit."

If anything, I could trust Arnold not to mince his words. I thought I had brushed up quite nicely but considering I had spent the last few days mostly in the dark, in my pyjamas, in bed, watching Netflix, eating junk food, and intermittently crying my heart out, I could hardly have expected anything else.

"Clearly, being a lady of leisure is not agreeing with you."

"Come in, Arnold," I said, and waved him into my flat. "I got your favourite king prawns." I changed the topic to food, since Arnold was on a perpetual diet. A few years ago, he had jumped onto the Keto bandwagon and was now a complete Keto evangelist.

"Oh, honey, I'm so sorry. I won't be staying for lunch. I have a meeting with Steve at the Oxo in half an hour."

I knew Steve was their new partner at the law firm and I also knew that Arnold had a hard-on the size of the Oxo Tower itself for said Steve.

"Did you book a room?"

"Bitchy. I was right that being a lady of leisure clearly has done you no good."

To be fair, just because I was miserable and had my heart broken, I didn't need to be foul to Arnold, who has been so faithful and done so much for me over the years.

"Sorry" was all I said.

He headed towards the living room. On passing the kitchen counter and seeing the large spread of canapès and snacks that I had ordered for our lunch, he let out a wolf whistle.

"Had I known you were going to put on such a spread, I would have told Steve to meet me here."

I rolled my eyes. He was just being nice and I knew he was in a hurry.

"So, where do I need to sign?" I picked up a large plate of prawns and moved it to the sink.

Arnold immediately took out the documents and a pen and laid them out in the space I had cleared on the counter.

"Here, here, and here." He pointed at the various places on the documents.

I signed and returned his pen. Within minutes, I saw him out the front door. As lovely as he was, I was not in the mood for niceties and I felt relieved I had been spared from having to entertain anyone.

As I returned to the living room, I realised that now I truly had nothing and no one. I was a complete free agent, free to drift like a satellite out of orbit, and I felt completely lost. I stopped and bit back another bout of tears.

There was a knock at the door. Arnold must have forgotten something. I went to open it.

"Let me guess, you forgot your chastity belt." The words died on my lips.

In front of me stood Jacko.

I don't know how much time passed as I stood there staring, unable to believe my eyes.

Eventually Jacko spoke. "Can I come in?"

I couldn't trust my voice. I stepped aside.

Jacko was dressed in beige corduroys, a white shirt, and a suede jacket, looking casually cool with her dark tan, dark hair and dark eyes, fresh from the island. She probably turned heads on every corner wherever she went in pale, insipid London.

"Wow, nice place," she said, looking around.

It occurred to me then that Jacko had never been to my flat. I guessed that even countless hours of video calls would not do the reality of the space justice.

Her eyes landed on the luscious spread on my kitchen island.

"Are you expecting a football team for lunch? I know Arsenal just won the FA Cup, but I never took you for a football fan."

I was glad to see her sense of humour had returned since our last encounter. I didn't trust it, though. But I managed to find my voice. "What brings you here?"

She turned, glanced out the window and shoved her hands in her corduroy pockets in that way that I had seen her do with her shorts. It seemed really strange to see her now in trousers.

"That," she said slowly, "is an enormous question. One we probably need to talk about in some detail but the short answer is simple." Jacko looked at me, her eyes piercing and steady. "You."

It felt like she was speaking a different language. In fact, everything about the situation felt alien. This person in front of me was Jacko, yet she was not my usual Jacko. My heart cringed at the thought of my Jacko. After what had happened, she would never be my Jacko.

"You just travelled from Greece via, let me see, that would be bus, ferry, three trains, and probably the Eurostar to come to London, a journey that would take three days at best?"

Jacko nodded. Then she shook her head, none of which helped clarify anything.

"Actually, the journey took seven and a half hours door to door, to my hotel room at the Rose & Crown."

I frowned. Nothing was making sense at all.

"The flight was only four hours long. Thank God."

Had I just stepped into an alternate universe? "You flew?"

"Yes, and I survived. Who knew?" She shrugged.

I needed a drink. I went to my kitchen and poured a glass of wine. I took a large swig and noticed that Jacko's eyes were still on me. I took out another glass and slid it across the table towards her, along with the bottle.

"Help yourself and then it might be a good idea to start from the beginning and explain why you're here."

Jacko poured herself a glass, followed me, and sat down on the edge of the couch a little way from me. She carefully put her glass down on the coffee table, without taking a sip.

I, on the other hand, had glugged down a couple of large gulps before I settled, and waited for her to speak.

"The night after you left was a very bad night. The morning after was even worse because I was not only an emotional wreck, but I also had a hangover from hell. On my way to the pharmacy to get headache tablets, I, of course, bumped into Beers."

The mention of Beck's name brought a shiver to my spine. I took another swig of my wine.

"We had coffee and then some lunch and, of course, some drinks and, yes, afterwards, I took her back to mine." Jacko hesitated. "The point is, we ended up in bed."

Now was my turn to hold up a hand in a similar fashion to what Jacko did the night I left. "Please, spare me."

Jacko nodded. "The point is this. In the early hours of the

following morning, after spending a lot of time with Becks, I was about to curl up and go to sleep with her. I turned on my side and pulled her in towards me, as one would a lover, and I said good night."

I stared at Jacko, still unable to understand what any of this had to do with me and why she was telling me this. Could this be a super-vindictive side of Jacko? I didn't want to believe that.

Eventually, she sighed and looked at me, holding my gaze. "I said, 'I love you...Spice.'"

Jacko picked up her glass and took a gulp, averting her eyes. "The point is, the words tumbled out of me before I realised what I'd said."

I was holding my breath. Those were four words I thought I would never hear, let alone find out that Jacko had accidentally said them to the wrong lover.

"Of course, that was the wrong thing to say, and Beers left shortly afterwards and I haven't seen her since."

I felt the anger bubble up inside. "So, now that you fucked it up with her, you thought you'd come and have me?" Again, the words tumbled out of my mouth before I could stop them. I had no defences left.

Jacko shook her head. For some unknown reason, she smiled at me. I could not understand what she could possibly find amusing. Behind that smile, I saw both utter sadness and something else.

"Not at all, Spice. I heard what you said when you left. At first, I didn't believe it. But when that happened that night with Becks, I realised the truth for me, too. The person I wanted—want—in my bed... is you."

I instinctively shook my head, scared that this might be a bad joke.

"The person I've been hankering after for years is you. Every person I meet, every girl I like, I compare to you. For as long as I can remember... I think it's always been you. But I've been blind, or scared, and then the realisation that I might have lost you forever made me wake up. I realised that losing you was my greatest fear. Even bigger than flying. And I decided that not even the terror of getting into a plane was going to keep me from seeing you and telling you how I feel."

I reacted on impulse. I grabbed my empty glass and headed to the sink, where I refilled it with cold water from the tap. I needed my brain to work. I drank down a few gulps, buying myself time.

Could this possibly be true?

Was Jacko just fucking with me to get revenge?

I watched over the rim of my glass as she came towards me at the kitchen island.

"Now, I know this is all a lot to take in, Spice. I also realise that you might not want anything to do with me, or not want the same thing I do anymore, so I have booked myself into the hotel for the next week to give you time to absorb what I've said and to think it through. I hope in the interest of our years as best friends, you will do me that huge favour, at least to think things through, despite my exceedingly bad and rude behaviour the last time I saw you." Jacko took a step towards me.

I placed my glass on the table. I turned towards her, wanting to give her a piece of my mind. Instead, her dark eyes and the warmth of her body so close to me overwhelmed me and I leant in and kissed her.

That was the only answer she needed.

That was the only answer we both needed.

EPILOGUE

*M*y bones felt like they were made of rubber. I hadn't felt this giddy since my hormonal teens, when I had almost swooned over a girl crush. Girl crushes, for that matter. It was truly amazing what one would endure—correction, could thoroughly enjoy. Because, this time, love was involved and even more so spice. Yes, that kind of spice!

Since Jacko arrived on my doorstep, sleep has not been a high priority. I can feel my cheeks blush just at the thought.

Although I am under slept, and know at some point we will probably crash, I feel good, excited, happy and, like I could tackle the world. We have done well.

As you know, it has taken me, if you count the really rocky restarts —first, the deep water of denial, and then the major, be it unintentional fuck-up with Becks, the better part of three months to get here.

The largest world-crushing moment came the night I left Eressos, when Jacko would not even look at me. I still get the shudders just thinking about it. I really had not experienced such sadness and devastation, not even when I thought I was going to lose my precious business. No, it was not touch and go. I honestly thought I had lost everything.

Behind me, Jacko cleared her throat.

I turned to find her standing in the doorway of my bedroom, looking dashing in a midnight blue tailored tuxedo and crisp white wing collar shirt. My mouth went dry and my heart almost stopped.

"You look lovely," she said before I could speak.

I got up from the dressing table where I had been putting on my makeup. I did a little twirl in my cobalt blue silk satin frock and heals. I must confess I very rarely wear dresses and heals but on this occasion, it called for something special. Her Russian oligarch's daughter had brought one of the Stradivari to London on a very rare mini tour, and Jacko and her plus one were to be guests of honour at the Royal Albert Hall. I was to be her plus one.

Jacko just stood there, casually leaning against the door frame, with that silly lopsided grin on her face, studying me. The way she made me feel when she did that—like I was the only person in the world. I might as well have been but naked since she was staring into my soul.

I walked over to her and slid my hands around her narrow waist and kissed her. "So do you," I whispered.

"Ready?" She turned and offered me her arm.

I smiled at the overly chivalrous gesture. "Probably not," I said and slid my arm through hers.

IF YOU ENJOYED THIS...

1) Reviews are one of the most important ways for authors to gain visibility and bring their books to the attention of interested readers.

If you've enjoyed this book, please leave a review on your favourite reader platforms. It can be as short as you like and need only take a few minutes but would really mean a lot.

PLEASE NO SPOILERS! It ruins the reading experience for other readers.

Jump to your favourite reader platform now >>

Alternatively, send me feedback here:

mail@SamSkyborne.com

Thank you very much!

---

2) To be notified of future releases and receive writing related news, please

JOIN MY VIP READER CLUB

http://SamSkyborne.com/Signup

This is a spam free zone, used exclusively to keep in touch with VIP readers.

---

3) Turn the page to see other books you might also like…

BY SAM SKYBORNE

LESVOS ISLAND COLLECTION (ROMANCE)

Sealed with a Kiss

The Sappho Romance *(Alt. Hist. spinoff)*

A Change of Heart

Eye of the Storm

Sugar and Spice

Amenah Awakens*

SHORT STORIES

Unbroken* (Steampunk Romance)

Milton Meets Her Match

The Yellow Tandem

Stakeout

Love in the Time of COVID

LESBIAN EROTIC SHORTS (L.E.S) STORY & FILM

Cat Sitting: Lesbian Cat Custody Complications

Saying Sorry: A Queer & Complex Process

---

* Free to VIP Reader Club.

See back of book for details >>

BY S.M. SKYBORNE

TONI MENDEZ SERIES (LESBIAN PI THRILLER)

RISK: Three Crime-fighting Women Risk All for Love, Lust and Justice

Project ALICE

Starting Over*

———————————

Free to VIP Reader Club.

See back of book for details >>

BY JACQUIE LYON

ALT HISTORY FICTION

The Sappho Romance

The Songs of Bilitis (Translated by)

ABOUT

"The sky is merely the start..."

Sam Skyborne is the proud author of a number of award winning novels and currently lives & loves in London (UK) while happily going on writing adventures across the globe ... or as far as the mind will travel.

Connect with Sam:

Join Sam's Reader Club: http://SamSkyborne.com/Signup

Private Facebook Reader Group:
Facebook.com/groups/SamSkyborneGroup

Facebook Page: @SamSkybornePage

Instagram: @SamSkyborne

YouTube: @SamSkyborneAuthor

Sam's online home: SamSkyborne.com

Or drop Sam an email: mail@SamSkyborne.com

ACKNOWLEDGEMENTS

A wise author once said:

> "Even though writing a book starts off as a solitary endeavour, to finish a book takes the dedication, hard work and kindness of a small but substantial army."

So with that in mind, I'd very much like to thank my little army—my editorial team, my friends and family. I could not have done this without you.

Special thanks to Emmanuel for having such a lovely house in which I could incubate and complete the final draft of this story.

Last but not least, thank you to my loyal readers. You are the reason I do this.

Printed in Great Britain
by Amazon